A Beautiful Lack
of Consequence

ALSO BY MONIKA RADOJEVIC

Teeth in the Back of My Neck (poems)

A Beautiful Lack of Consequence

Monika Radojevic

#MERKY BOOKS

UK | USA | Canada | Ireland | Australia
India | New Zealand | South Africa

#Merky Books is part of the Penguin Random House group of companies
whose addresses can be found at global.penguinrandomhouse.com

Penguin Random House UK,
One Embassy Gardens, 8 Viaduct Gardens, London SW11 7BW

penguin.co.uk

Penguin
Random House
UK

First published 2025
001

Typeset in 13.3/15.8pt Garamond MT Std by Jouve (UK), Milton Keynes
Printed and bound in Great Britain by Clays Ltd, Elcograf S.p.A.

The authorised representative in the EEA is Penguin Random House Ireland,
Morrison Chambers, 32 Nassau Street, Dublin D02 YH68

A CIP catalogue record for this book is available from the British Library

ISBN: 978-1-529-91871-7

For the girls. Always the girls.

'For all women must destroy in order to create.'
Myra Jehlen, *Readings at the Edge of Literature*

Contents

CONTENTS

Salt Badgers

Anya was woken by the sound of dishes clattering to the floor, immediately followed by wailing. In fact, she thought she heard glass break. She scrambled for the baseball bat she kept by her bed, even though they all knew she would never use it, and shook Mark awake as she ran for the door.

'Again?' he groaned, pulling the skin of his face down with his palms. Still, he dutifully followed her into the kitchen, yanking open the back door and helping her chase several of the creatures out into the garden. It was too dark to see where they went, but he heard their indignant little grunts as they scurried away from the yellow light. He looked back at his girlfriend's strained face, puffy from tiredness, and wished he had something better to offer.

'That's the third time this week,' he said, as she began to sweep up the water glass they'd knocked over. Anya felt tears of exhaustion prickle her eyes and angrily blinked them away, throwing the shards into the bin. It was also their fifth glass of the week. Things were getting expensive.

The salt badgers had started terrorising them six months ago. Anya knew why they'd been targeted. She'd turned thirty in November, with her womb still empty – much to her relief – and they'd arrived a week later. Mark rolled his eyes whenever she brought it up, but Anya was certain that's what kept the badgers there. Even if the science was inconclusive. Even if the government's official line was that they struck at random, and that retaliation was highly illegal, punishable by up to life in prison. In every account of a salt badger outbreak, they had only ever gone away when someone fell pregnant. *Nothing* else worked.

The thing about salt badgers is that they were a nuisance. No matter which way you looked at it. Anya knew their existence was vital to humanity, that their exploited ecosystem was fragile enough already, et cetera et cetera. The badgers' salt caves, scattered across multiple continents and protected by a multinational institution – although everyone knew they were in America's pocket – were precious enough to spark a world war. School had taught her that salt badgers and humans had lived harmoniously for millennia. But faced with the grim reality of the occupation of *her own flat*, part of her wondered whether it was all propaganda. She had become jumpy and irritable in the months after the badgers arrived, constantly harangued by their noise, their mess, their demands for food. If she didn't feed them, they'd start eating the furniture and getting sick. And if they ended up with a dead body in their home, the police would investigate. Their cat, Clementine, had transformed into an outdoor cat almost overnight, rarely entering the home, and Anya missed the way she used to curl between her and Mark's heads in bed, often licking their hair in the mornings. The badgers shed too, *everywhere*. It didn't seem to matter how often she or Mark dragged the vacuum out, the fur got into the weirdest places – like inside the oven.

At least they were cute, despite their stink and the trail of little dead creatures – usually mice – that followed them around. When they first appeared, the badgers growled and snapped whenever they got too close, but eventually Anya could cradle one and bury her face in it, if she wanted to. Not that she would – they rarely smelt good, like ammonia and rotting leaves. Each badger was roughly the size of a human hand, with incredibly soft fur – either greyish, a light pink or black, depending on the salt they produced. They had the classic white stripes and whiskers, and were entirely unafraid of Anya and Mark, often brushing up against them and asking to be stroked, or even held. Once, she and Mark had been in the middle of lovemaking and he'd yelped in pain as one of the badgers had bitten his foot, drawing blood.

'I'm . . . I'm having trouble concentrating at the moment,' Anya told Roberta the next day over Zoom. She'd informed her boss when the badgers had first arrived, of course, insisting that it wouldn't affect her work – because why should they? Anya had initially seen the badgers and her work as two entirely separate entities, different planets in the solar system of her life. She'd even said something along those lines to Roberta. But now, consumed and exhausted by the badgers, the words curdled in her mouth. She disliked how naive and eager they had made her sound, even though her boss had nodded slowly, as if Anya had said something profound. And at first, Roberta had been empathetic, telling her what she had to look forward to and offering helpful tips to badger-proof her home. 'They'll chew on any kind of carpet or loose fabric,' she'd said, 'so you might want to consider hardwood floors.' They'd granted her the legally mandated two weeks of paid leave, giving her time to roll up and bag her beloved Persian rug and the hand-crocheted table runners her grandma had made for her before her death, and to give away the cheese plant (fatal if any badgers ingested the leaves). She and Mark had lugged home buckets of dry feed, setting them back hundreds of pounds. The shopkeeper had assured them they wouldn't need to come back for months, but their badgers either ate double the regular amount or she'd lied, because it seemed like they were having to drive to the pet store every other week. Neither she nor Mark had been given a pay rise, even though it was encouraged by the state, and they'd switched to working entirely online to try and make back the loss.

As the months rolled on, Anya noticed that her bosses had become less and less sympathetic about the havoc and instability the badgers were wreaking on her life. Mark's company seemed unbothered when he turned up to meetings a little dishevelled, having just fished a salt badger out of the toilet and made sure it was still breathing. He asked for, and was given, extensions on big projects, and didn't feel guilty about logging off at five – or half five at the latest. His work praised him for keeping it together despite the disruption. In fact – and

she tried hard not to resent him for this – a couple of
months ago when she'd returned from an overnight trip
for an urgent case, she'd found a goodie basket of wine,
coffee, shortbread and truffles with his name on it.

'They sent it to me for my time "single-parenting",'
Mark said sheepishly.

'Who did?' she asked with a mouth full of rose-
infused chocolate.

'The office.'

Anya had once walked into the kitchen, where Mark
worked, to find him and his Head of HR in hysterics
as a salt badger – a particularly fat one – struggled to
remove its head from an empty tube of Pringles it had
dug out of the recycling. On one of her rare days in the
office, Anya had relayed that story to her co-worker Julie,
laughing about it herself and showing her the video Mark
had filmed. But Julie hadn't laughed at all, pressing her
mouth into a white line and informing her that Pringles
could make the badgers sick, and *what was she thinking?*

Anya's work, though – it wasn't that they said
anything to her, it was much more subtle than that, constantly leaving her wondering if she was just reading into
things. When she politely turned down overtime, citing
the need to take the badgers to the vet for their weigh-
ins, she was met with a surprised silence that made her
feel like she'd fucked up, and was being judged for it.
Her lack of availability – especially in the evenings –
was treated like an inconvenience. One of the senior
partners commented that Anya seemed to be dressing
'more casually now' when she stopped blow-drying her

hair and wearing make-up. It was true that as a lawyer there was a certain professionalism required, whereas Mark worked in the charity sector. But she noticed meetings cropping up in co-workers' calendars that she wasn't invited to; cases being passed to other, badger-free colleagues even when she expressed an interest in taking them on. This was the first time she had admitted to Roberta that she was struggling, and she felt shrunken and ashamed for it.

'Huh,' Roberta said carefully. She paused for a bit, as if expecting Anya to fill the gap. When she didn't, Roberta sighed.

'I see. And is there anything that might be causing this? Anything work-related?'

'Well,' Anya pushed her glasses higher up the bridge of her nose, 'not exactly work-related, but I'm having a really hard time with the badgers. They've started teething, so they cry and keep coming into the kitchen at night—'

'You know, when I had the salties, I sectioned off a room in the house for them and kept them there,' Roberta interrupted. 'We got a minder in for a few days a week and I used those hours to really make sure I was on top of everything for the two other days when I had to go it alone. Have you given any thought to doing that?'

Anya smiled tightly. 'We don't have a spare room, unfortunately. We've got a basement flat . . . but I can talk to Mark about the minder, and see if it's an option for us. Financially.' It wasn't.

'It's really about using the times when they're asleep

to maximise your efficiency. Why don't you come back into the office a few more days a week?'

Anya found her eyes drifting, yet again, to her appearance in the camera preview. She'd got up earlier than usual to wash her hair and it had dried haphazardly, so she'd French-braided it to tone down the frizz. She hadn't thought she looked too bad, but compared to Roberta, who was immaculately dressed in a white pantsuit and deep crimson turtleneck, her hair in an elegant bun, she felt frumpy and lifeless. The mere thought of having to drag herself back to the office brought tears to her eyes. Not to mention that they would *still* have to pay for a minder, a fact her manager seemed determined to ignore.

'I guess I could, but what would actually help would be something a – a little more substantial. From the company.'

Her boss raised her eyebrows. 'The company?'

'I've talked to a few women at work, and I really think it could help boost productivity if there was a space within the office – or nearby – where we could safely leave the badgers during working hours for a discounted rate. Or – for free.'

Roberta's face was blank, and Anya felt her resolve crumbling. She glanced down at her keyboard for a moment. Then, avoiding eye contact, she stared at the dignified, floor-to-ceiling bookcase over her boss's shoulder, as she often did in their meetings. 'Or a subsidy programme we could enter into that would help with all the associated costs . . . or more flexible working hours.' She was painfully aware of how unconvincing she sounded. 'Being present and prepared for my job is really import- ant to me. If I had the option of starting a little later—'

'Your contracted hours are eight to five. Clients expect us to be reachable during that time, Anya. Or are you requesting a contract renegotiation?'

*

'How'd it go?' Mark asked when she headed into the kitchen to find something to eat. Most of the badgers were outside, sleeping in the sun, but one of them was snuffling around the room. It mewled in delight when Anya scooped it up in her arms and brought it to her chest.

'Terribly. She looked at me like I'd asked her to come over and watch the badgers herself.' Anya pushed a slice of bread into the toaster and grabbed the butter dish out of the fridge, holding it arm's-length away from the badger. 'How about you?'

He shrugged. 'They said they'd look into it. I don't think it will amount to anything. You know they've barely got the funds to keep the lights on.' He kissed the back of her neck as she leant against him and closed her eyes, feeling the badger's tiny heart hammering against her own.

*

It turned out to be the start of a disastrous week for Anya. She'd just about kept on top of cases by working through her lunch hours and well into the evenings, but on Wednesday morning she walked into the kitchen and froze, gagging at the stench. Two of the badgers had vomited an astonishing amount of orange gunk on to the floor, and were lying in the middle of it, their little chests rising and falling furiously. The smell was so awful she'd immediately thrown up into the sink, scrabbling for her phone as she wiped spit off her chin. To make matters worse, Mark was away with work and the usual vet wouldn't take them. 'It sounds like croup,' she told Anya, 'too contagious for me to accept. You'll need to go to St Francis, in Chelmsford.'

'That's over an hour away!'

'Well, I'd go quickly if I were you. If their condition is as bad as it sounds, they need urgent care. I'll call ahead and let them know you're coming.'

It was only after she'd lifted the stinking, shaking badgers into the carrier, strapped them into her car and pulled up at St Francis that Anya realised she'd left her phone at home, and had no way to let the office know she wasn't available. At first, she figured she could drop the badgers off and go back, grab her laptop, maybe even answer emails from the hospital. But when she tried to leave them, the veterinary nurse ran after her, grabbing her shoulder.

'I'm sorry, but you're legally responsible for your badgers and we need you to remain in the building at all times. There's also paperwork we need you to do, in case of death. By the way,' he'd added as she hunched over in the waiting-room chair, trying to remember her National Insurance number, 'due to staff shortages, there is currently a four-hour wait.'

By the time Anya got home it was almost six in the

evening, and she was faint with hunger. Her kitchen was still a disaster zone, and she could hear the remaining badgers mewling in the garden, enraged and starving after being neglected all day. The quietest room was the bathroom. She grabbed her phone and got into the empty bathtub, shoving dry crackers into her mouth. Seventy-three work emails (including two from HR), missed calls from Mark, a message from her friend Leonora wanting to know if she was coming to her hen party, and a single text from Roberta.

Call me immediately. Sent four hours ago.

'Shit.' Anya took a deep breath and pressed her back into the cold porcelain. Her boss picked up on the first ring.

'Anya. Where have you been? Has there been an accident?'

'I'm so sorry, Roberta, I had an emergency with two of my badgers – the vet thought it was croup – there's orange vomit all over my kitchen—' Anya's voice broke and she started sobbing, her face growing hot with humiliation. 'I'm so, so sorry for not calling in today. In my rush to get them to the hospital, I left my phone at home.'

'Are the badgers all right?' Roberta sounded stiff and clipped, and it only made Anya cry harder.

'They're fine. It's not even croup, they just have a bad case of worms, which they also happen to be allergic to. I have to pick them up tomorrow.' She sniffed loudly, and tried to get her breathing under control. A new, terrifying sensation was sliding along her spine, as though someone had dropped an ice cube down her back. What if they fired her for this?

Roberta let out a sigh. 'Oh, good! Glad to hear it. Always a scary thing when the little ones aren't well. But, Anya, I'm sorry to say that your behaviour today was rather unprofessional. I do completely understand you were dealing with a personal issue, but you *are* aware of our policies for sick days or emergencies, and a vital part of that policy is informing me when you know you're not going to be able to work.'

'I'm aware, Roberta, and again I can only apologise. It was a total accident. I thought my phone was in my pocket, and my plan was—'

'I'm reminding you because we have clients, Anya, who rely on us to protect and uphold their rights. Because you failed to inform us of your absence, no one knew you were missing until we received complaints from two clients – it's not really a look we can afford, frankly.'

Anya stared down at the crackers in her lap and wondered if she was going to be sick again. This was getting ridiculous. If they were going to fire her for an honest mistake, she was done being apologetic. 'In the five years I've worked with you, I've almost never taken a sick day, and to the best of my knowledge, I've never breached our policies either. I hope my track record can speak for itself, despite my error today.'

Roberta sighed again. 'Well, I appreciate that, Anya. Let's draw a line under this week. However, we've got to ensure this lapse of judgement doesn't happen again—'

'With all due respect, it wasn't a lapse in judgement.' Anya heard the tremor in her voice but was too exhausted and frustrated to care. 'I had an emergency and Mark isn't home at the moment, so I had to handle two sick badgers alone, as fast as I could. I thought they were in real danger, and in the rush I forgot my phone. I've already asked you for additional support because of my situation at home, and I'm asking you again, as I think today has made it clear that I'm not coping as well as I thought I was.'

A long pause, and Anya felt the fight drain from her. She suddenly wanted nothing more than to end the conversation. Hang up, lie in the bath and eat her crackers.

'Anya, thank you for your honesty. Now it's time for me to be honest. I agree that you're struggling at the moment. I've been toying with a performance improvement plan for you and I think it might—'

Anya's phone buzzed and she momentarily tuned Roberta out to read Mark's text. *Everything OK over there? I'm on my way home, back by nine. Want a curry?* Her vision blurred as her eyes filled with tears, while Roberta droned on and on in her ear.

In the hours before Mark arrived, Anya crushed tablets into the badgers' feed, cleaned all the vomit off the floor – gagging as she used toothpicks to scrape between the floorboards – and checked each badger for signs of an infestation. Glancing at her phone on her way to wash off the sweat and grime, she saw an email from Roberta.

Hi Anya,

On further reflection after our conversations, I unfortunately don't see any viable outcomes for your suggestions regarding badger care. The idea of using company funds to support your personal predicament is a little inappropriate, and I'd caution against raising this again, particularly after today's incident.

I will, however, speak to HR about switching your working hours to nine to six – although I'll still need you to attend the 8.30 meetings on Tuesdays, as shifting those would disrupt everyone else's work schedule. Does that sound like a good compromise?

I'll be putting a meeting in your calendar for Monday to discuss your performance improvement plan too, and we'll be joined by a HR rep to make sure we support you as much as we possibly can.

Over the next few months, I think you'd do well to focus on maximising your efficiency and perhaps setting up a schedule to ensure your clients have the one-on-one time with you they require. Woman to woman, I'd be happy to meet with you during work hours and help you figure this out, and hopefully we'll get you back on track soon.

Best,
R

Anya was woken by the sound of dishes clattering to the floor, immediately followed by wailing. In fact, she thought she heard glass break. She scrambled for the baseball bat. Mark swore as she shook him awake.

'Again?' he groaned, squinting at the overhead lights. Still, he dutifully followed her into the kitchen, yanking open the back door and helping her chase several of the creatures out into the garden. It was too dark to see where they went, but he heard their indignant little grunts as they scurried away. For a moment, they stood in the dark, listening. Then Mark flicked on the lights, and the strong smell of sulphur and shit suddenly made sense.

One of the badgers had shat on the floor and the rest of them had trodden in it, spreading it across the wood and kitchen tile. They could see it was fresh and peppered with chunks of dark green slime. Shards of glass and blood from the badgers' feet could be tracked all the way to the garden door. It was a miracle that neither Anya nor Mark had stepped in any of it themselves.

Anya turned to Mark and wondered whether she looked depleted and numb in his eyes. Or tearful. Or furious. Truthfully, she did not know how she felt. She was struck by two urges: to laugh, or to turn and go back to her bed, shutting the kitchen door behind her and letting Mark get down on his hands and knees with the toothpicks and the dustpan and brush. She could see guilt on his face. Even though Anya knew none of this was his fault, seeing him look at her like that – as if he were waiting for instructions – infuriated her. She stared at the gleaming brown smears, and willed herself not to start shouting.

'I'll clean it,' Mark said, too hastily. 'You did the vomit—'

'It's fine. We'll do it together. Quickly.' She tried to keep the impatience from her voice as she moved to the cupboard under the sink and tossed him the packet of disposable gloves. But Anya had never been very good at throwing. They sailed across the room, too low and haphazard for Mark to catch, landing wetly, perfectly, in the warm mound of shit.

Real Mothers

Oh . . . You've just woken up? On a Saturday afternoon? Ah, I see! Up since seven, then – that's nearly as early as me! Any kids, d'you mind me asking? Two? Ah, two girls? They're so cute, aren't they, when they're tiny. I've got two of my own. One's off at university, but my youngest, Bertie, is still at home. She's named after her nan, because they look the same – you wouldn't believe it! Bertie got Mum's beautiful thick hair, nothing like the sad excuse on my head . . .When I braid it for her, she practically glows. Do your girls go to St Morley's? Or are they too young? Oh, they do! What year? Ah, so a few years below my Bertie, then – I thought I recognised your face, I'm sure I must have seen you around at one of the bake sales or the tombolas! Ah, I knew it! It was a fantastic night, wasn't it? I can't believe we hit the target. Twenty thousand pounds – I really didn't think we'd do it. Have your girls had a chance to test out the new kiln yet? Ah, that's a shame. Bertie too, it's not really her thing. She's really into her history, always has her nose buried in a book – even at the dinner table!

Anyway, I know you must be terribly busy, I won't take a moment of your time – wouldn't dream of bothering a hard-working mum like yourself on a sunny afternoon like this one! I've been knocking on the doors talking to all the parents in the area because I'm not sure if you've heard. Of the latest? The Jenson girl? No? Oh, darling, I'm so sorry to be the one to tell you the news. They've found her jumper. Yes. Yes, they have. I know. Isn't it just? So terrible. She's the third girl to disappear in my time living here, although the police have said there's no evidence of foul play. Yet. Suppose she could have run away . . . girls are dramatic at that age, aren't they? But until she's been found safe and sound, I can't relax. It makes my blood boil. Doesn't it make your blood boil? What was your name again, darling? I didn't catch it the first time round.

Nadia. *Such* a beautiful name. My mother was called Nadia, Nadia Ambreen. Ambreen was her middle name. But we always called her Bertie – and, of course, I named my youngest after her.

Listen, Nadia, about the Jenson girl. Evie, Evie Jenson. I'm really worried, Nadia. Terribly worried. I've been worried since Anna-Marie, in 2017, and Paula, in 2003. I'm a stay-at-home mum myself. I've got my Bertie to think about, when she goes out with her friends or when she's coming back from school. She's only fourteen but she seems so much older . . . it worries me terribly, Nadia. That's why I'm here, actually, to talk to you about some of the products my husband's company has been making – it's ridiculous, they've been trying to get a contract from the government to try and mass-distribute these in schools, but the Home Secretary, that Martin guy, he's not budging. Says they're just going to put in more street lights, but not even in our borough . . . I know. They're all just a bit useless, aren't they?

Anyway, darling, I said I wouldn't take up much of your time, didn't I? So let me just tell you upfront why I'm here. I want to talk to you – and all the mums in the area – about my husband – Darren – and his products. Because like I said, now that they aren't getting these contracts, they're going to start selling them online and on Amazon and all those places. Darren's team have a meeting with Sainsbury's to get it in the bigger shops – exciting, isn't it? In the meantime, I thought I'd go talk to women who are actually the ones in danger, because, well, Darren's team are all lovely but the ones that matter are men! All of them! Darren says they've done market research and gotten all this great customer feedback, but I just don't think it's right that they're not speaking to real women – *real mothers* – like us, to test out all the products. When our girls are at risk and no one's getting to the root of the problem, we women have to stick together. And mothers always know best, right? I mean, some of these products really are fantastic – and because you'd basically be doing me a favour by trying them out, I'm offering you a third off, just for today. And really, who knows when they'll be online anyway? Half the time Bertie wants to buy something online, it's sold out or it never arrives! They do that very cheeky thing where they take a picture of the doorstep, or something random, and they mark it as delivered, don't they? But that could be anyone's floor! And then it's impossible to get your money back – isn't it the most frustrating thing?

Let me tell you about what I'd love to show you today. We've got three products – and remember, I'm giving you a third off! Just for today! Okay, let's just get them out for you, then. They're all packaged up neatly . . . one sec . . . I'm still out of breath from climbing up your gorgeous front steps!

Here we go, Nadia. I am *thrilled* to present to you the Anti-Surprise Earring Set: for when doing everything right just isn't enough. Imagine this, darling.

You're walking back from the train station, it's eleven thirty at night. The route you usually take, the shortcut, is badly lit and deserted at this hour. So, you take the long way home, bag tucked into your elbow, keys in one hand, phone in the other. You've texted ahead that you're walking back, you've got your keypad up in case you need to call for help. You've changed out of your heels, even though it was inconvenient to bring a second pair of shoes with you. It meant you had to pay to check your bag in at the concert – how annoying! Now, darling, you're walking fast but not too fast, alert but not attention-seeking. Your heart is pounding, your blood is singing – you know what I mean, don't you? The way your entire body is tense, your movements jerky and too quick, adrenaline rushing through your veins. That's probably what those poor girls felt, just before they vanished. Every noise, every snap of a twig or rustle of a bush, makes you jump in fear. You realise you're narrating your own attack, imagining what you'd do to escape or how you'd try to fight back. Yes, it's a bit creepy – but the better prepared you are the better your chances are of making it home safely. You glance behind you as you're about to cross the road and THERE HE IS. He's crept up behind you so quietly you didn't catch it, he's closing the gap, he's reaching out, you're frozen – BOOM.

Here you go, darling: hold them in your hands and

give them a feel. Light as a feather, aren't they? We have to face the facts, don't we, darling? A woman is killed every 2.5 days by a man. Yes, yes, you're right, it's usually a man she knows, but my husband's products are handy for every dangerous situation, because they're designed for everyday use. The trick is, you gotta be ready to die – I mean, to fight! – at any moment.

I can see you're still unsure. Let me see if I can convince you. In this country, a third of young girls and women are sexually harassed while using public transport, and 92 per cent of women have experienced street harassment in their lifetime, which includes flashing and groping. *Groping*, darling. Disgusting. The world is not safe for us, not built for us, not changing fast enough for us.

We need to do everything we can to tip the scales in our favour. Which is why I think you'd be really interested in the sterling silver Anti-Surprise Set – I'll give you the science behind it, and stop wittering on!

As you can see, these seem like a classic feminine set of pearl earrings. Although, of course, they're suitable for everyone – no matter how you identify – because we've got a range of sizes and colours, and we're working on a clip-on version of these for girls – well, for anyone – who haven't got their ears pierced.

Ah – I'm so glad you asked! If you look closely, you can see the fastening of our Anti-Surprise Set is a little bulkier than you'd expect, right? Don't worry, though; if you cup it the way you're doing now, again, you can feel how lightweight they are, right? They won't stretch

your earlobes at all! That little bulky bit that looks like a
screw head is actually a built-in sensor that alerts you if
someone is behind you, so no one can ever sneak up on
you! Look – feel that little pulse. Quite a strong vibra-
tion, right? When it's on your ear, the sensation is even
stronger and immediately focuses your attention on any
potential threat. The closer he is, the stronger the pulse,
and it senses up to ten metres behind you, so you have
time to react.

And I know what you're thinking. *Wouldn't these be
impossible in a crowd?* Or, what if it picked up literally
everything behind you – a bin, a fox, a child? Well, that's
the *real* genius of these little things. First of all, they
only pick up moving objects, and they've been calibrated
to the average male height, with a 10 per cent leeway
either way. That was my idea. Secondly – and personally, this is what I really love about them – you can turn
them *on and off* when needed! Yes! If you twist them to
the right, the sensor shuts off so you can move through
a crowd peacefully if you prefer.

No, no charging needed, because when their two-
hour battery drains, the earrings charge up with your
movements. Kinetic, Darren says. That's right, they con-
tinuously charge *as you walk*, so you'll never find yourself
feeling helpless walking down a dark street ever again.

It's pretty smart, isn't it? I can see from your face that
you're curious. We offer our Anti-Surprise Set in sterling
silver, eighteen-carat gold and a beautiful rose gold too.
And remember, I'm offering you an exclusive discount
for today only.

Ah, I see. What age did you say your girls were again? Twelve and fourteen? Yes, I can see that they may be a little young for these – although they'd make a great first-year university gift, wouldn't they? All those nightclubs. But anyway, I've got the perfect thing to keep your girls safe in and out of school. God. D'you remember that poor Pointer girl? Paula, Paula Pointer, in 2003. He grabbed her by the hair. In fact, Darren's research team have found that baggy jumpers, loose hair and long scarves are the first things to be grabbed in 13 per cent of street attacks, because it's harder for our girls to get away – and that's the fashion these days, isn't it? Baggy this and oversized that. Bertie's always buying clothes two sizes too big, drives me up the wall, especially because I can't bear to creep over a size 12. Not all of us can have that gorgeous tiny little waist of yours, darling – in fact, that's why I think this one might be for you. Now, imagine this.

You're out for your morning jog, 6 a.m. I knew you'd be a jogger, with a figure like that! It's bright, a few cars on the road, but you cut into the park for your route and your earphones are blasting . . . oh, let's say Madonna!

The park is quiet at this time of the day. You run past a few dog owners clutching their nasty little poo bags and on to the open field by the train station, to do a lap. You're so focused on the pace, on Madonna honking in your ear, that you don't even realise he's behind you, grabbing at you, until it's happened. But here's the thing, darling! Your gilet! It's made of the latest glass-cut steel microfibres, triple-coated with solarium. Solarium – you know it? The world's slipperiest material, sustainably sourced from seaweed, and toxin-free! It gives off that sheen, like an oil spill. Brilliant stuff. And you've got an entire waistcoat of it; lightweight, keeping you warm, but breathable enough to wick away sweat. And it's slick. So slick his fingers can't get enough grip to properly grab you, giving you time to spin around and – here's the best bit, I think! – activate the refillable pepper spray sachet sewn into the lining!

It's activated with a quick press and twist of the little button on the breast pocket, so your attacker gets a faceful of potent pepper spray which renders him immobile and unable to see as you get away! BOOM!

Solarium, darling, it's so slippery I've got to hold the jacket by these handy little togs we've added on to the shoulders. Now, the thing I'm proudest of here is that little bit of plastic sewn in above the pepper spray button. That was my idea! I said to Darren that the problem with spray – having used it myself – is that if the wind is wrong it blows right back into your face! And THEN what happens? You're both there with your eyes streaming and unable to see! So, he went off and designed this little flap which acts as a visor and protects your face.

I know what you're thinking: *how on earth would that tiny little flap protect my face?* It's all to do with the angle of the spray, see. Let me just slip it on for you. Feels nice, doesn't it? Very luxe! I'll do a little demonstration – don't worry, it's just water! See, when I hold and twist . . . *there.* See how the visor acts as an effective shield? And this breast-pocket strip is a cotton-poly blend, not solarium, which means you've got the grip you need to hold and twist with one hand, if you need to. We've thought of everything, darling.

Both my girls have got these hanging in their wardrobes. I make them wear them whenever they're going somewhere a little dodgy. When they're walking to and from school, that sort of thing. We're developing new styles and colours too, but that's a little way off. Solarium isn't the cheapest material! We've got a really fitted style, though, as you can see, but you can easily size up if you want to layer up underneath, as a lot of our customers want to do.

Have a feel of that material. Gorgeous, right, Nadia? Easy to drop, isn't it! Machine washable? Absolutely, but no more than thirty. I actually do mine at twenty to be on the safe side – don't want that sheen coming off. The girls really like theirs, which shocked me, to be honest. I thought I'd have to fight to get them to wear it out, but they really like the idea of not being grabbable, of having time to get away.

Between you and me, I think Bertie likes how it protects her bra strap from the boys at school. Yes, you've heard too, haven't you. Disgusting things, trying to unhook the girls' bras when they're in the playground. Bertie told me one of them did it to her in art class last Friday, even scraping her skin a little because he was so rough with it. I've got half a mind to complain to the school, but in the meantime I've written to them and said I want her to be able to wear her waistcoat at all times of the day, just to be safe. Can't be too cautious, can we? I saw something in the news that said two thirds of young girls have some kind of unwanted sexual experience before they turn sixteen, and it's all happening at school. I don't even know how I'm going to talk to Bertie about it. Or Sara, my eldest.

Ah, wonderful! We'd be looking at five hundred pounds for two, and that's with the discount, remember!

I know, it's not cheap, is it? It's the solarium. What I *can* offer, though, is a size-swap scheme, so as your girls grow, you can exchange their waistcoats for a size or two up, so it's a lifetime purchase. Yes, even if they're ratty or stained. We recycle the material, you see, clean it up and repurpose it, because of the solarium. Good for your wallet, good for the planet. Shall I set a couple aside for you and you can have a think? Just remember, without the discount it would be close to seven hundred, so you really would be saving – oh fantastic, Nadia! Great decision, really. You're making a really smart decision for your girls.

Oh, you want one too! No, no, darling, you'd be a small/medium at the most, don't be silly! That tiny waist! TINY! Have a try of this one – and we've got silver too, if black isn't for you.

Oh, my. I know I'm biased but it really does suit you. I'd go black, personally, just so it goes with everything you have.

Yes, for three I can shave just a little more off – but I'm doing you a favour, one St Morley's mum to another! For three I'll take seven hundred, that's an extra fifty off *on top* of the discount.

Did you want to see my final product? It's a necklace that tracks the girls' heart rates, sends you text messages if it shoots up to abnormal levels and lets you pinpoint their loca— Of course, not a problem, Nadia, I completely understand! It's quite enough spending for one Saturday, isn't it! Of course, of course. No, you're not being rude, darling!

Doing this job and working with Darren, sometimes I can be a little blasé about it all, I know. It's a lot to think about, keeping yourself and your girls safe. All the things we do, the precautions we take. In a perfect world we wouldn't be buying all these things for our daughters – wouldn't need any solarium at all! – but until we get there, I'll be here. Giving us all one extra layer of safety for the mind and body.

Cash is preferable, Nadia darling, but if you've not got it, I have my machine somewhere in here. Just a moment.

While that's going through, let me show you a photo . . . that's my Darren, and that's Bertie tucked under his arm on the left, and Sara on the other side. My world. I never told you how we got started, did I? Darren founded the company when he got made redundant from his old job at Barclays – nice little package they gave him – and he was looking for an exciting new challenge. Turns out, the self-defence industry is *really* popular these days, and it's only going to get bigger! It's a new but growing market – I think that's what drew Darren to it, uncharted waters and all that. And of course, he wants to do his bit to help protect our girls from those horrible predators. He'd give all these products away for free if he could! Something to aim for, eh?

Brave Young Thing

Sakura blinks several times into the camera, a half-smile fixed on to her face. A very little half-smile. Almost like she doesn't even realise she's doing it. She must make her mouth as tiny as possible. Her chin is tilted, down and a little to the left. She's wearing no make-up, and this is rare, so she's anticipating an enthusiastic crowd. This one should be popular.

She's kneeling gracefully on the floor. Next to her is an empty glass. Just minutes before, it had been filled with chia seeds and water. Dinner. She moves it out of shot. Her nails, painted a creamy pink, are stamped with Hello Kitty stickers, and on each thumb she sports a diamanté version with pink whiskers. She looks like a pale, lithe fifteen-year-old. Silver glitter adorns her collarbones, and she's stuck a jade hairpin into her wig. In the camera lens, she can see the fairy lights reflected behind her, adorning the silk Japanese flag she had custom-made: the centre sun a dusky pink, cranes hand-stitched along the borders. The camera placement has to be meticulous; too far to the left and the light from the window will ruin the soft, pinkish glow created by her overpriced lighting rig. Too far to the right will reveal her bedroom door and remind the audience of Sakura's life beyond their screens. She's had tape marking the exact position of her Nikon on her carpet for years now. There are newish Post-it notes on the floor, their sticky strips already fluffing up with dirt. She whispers the words on them, perfecting the pronunciation; this part of her ritual. Live in three, two, *one*.

'*Hiiiiii*, everyone!' Sakura breathes, waggling her fingers. She glances behind her to double-check the door is locked, then settles back, watching the viewer count grow and the comments flicker in, careful not to let her smile slip. Watching the viewer count is the best part of her day, the fizz of excitement more potent than any alcoholic drink – not that she'd ever let her followers know she drank, of course. In these moments, Sakura is untouchable.

The compliments that roll in are meticulously counted too, the praise for her slim nose and flat, exposed midriff. A pale, slender girl-woman. How *boring*, how *predictable*, you might think. But she's not like that. Sakura is complex. You'll see.

She forces out a girlish giggle and checks the line of products arranged in front of her. 'I'll wait until there are a few more of you before I get started . . . so ask me anything!' She rests back on her knees again. 'Can you guys believe I've been doing this for *four* years now? It's like, so crazy how much time has passed, you know? Because, like, when I started, I had, like . . . three hundred Blossoms making up the fan base, and now I've got half a million of you. It's wild. My journey here is really thanks to you guys – that's why I love doing lives like these! It just feels way more intimate and special than, like, an edited video.'

The kind of comment she likes catches her attention and Sakura reads it out. 'Are you half?' She smiles, squinting her eyes into little crescent moons, and shrugs her shoulders.

'*Hai!* Half and proud!' she tells her audience. 'My mom is Japanese and my dad is from the States. Although, you know . . . I really think we should watch our language. Half implies I'm somehow not Japanese *or* American enough, y'know? I'm wholly both. Just saying.' She scrunches her nose cutely. Feels special, feels like she could just about cry from the adoration pouring out through her screen.

Another comment immediately pops up and Sakura's face changes. She flicks her gaze up to the camera's monitor, flipped round to face her, and stares directly into the lens. Her anger is so gorgeous – she could sell it.

'Yellow fever? Wow, really? I'm not going to tolerate racism on my own livestream, okay? You're out.' She blocks the user with a small twinge of satisfaction as outraged fans rush to her defence.

Sakura takes her Blossoms – the majority of them tweens – through her updated beauty routine. She pivoted to beauty and teen content early on in her career, when she identified the untapped spending potential of middle-class teenagers. In some ways, she's a pioneer, taking the girls seriously enough to gear her entire business towards them. As she demonstrates her favourite technique for applying concealer, she keeps an eye on the comment section, thanking the fans for their heartfelt messages decrying the racism she is subjected to on a daily basis.

'Hashtag StopAsianHate,' Sakura reads out at one point, nodding vigorously. 'You guys get it.' She's careful to keep her stomach sucked in, to keep her voice high-pitched, even though it makes her throat ache. She giggles a lot, sprinkling Japanese words into her instruc-tions and occasionally pretending to forget her English. It bores her, yes, this element of the job. But the pan-dering works *so well*. She tracks her likes and follows and shares obsessively, finding it soothing to measure just how loved she can make herself.

'Blossoms, help me out!' Sakura holds up an eyelash curler. 'What's this thing called again?' She squeals with laughter when the answer floods the comment section. 'God, you guys are so smart! Everyone says fifteen-year-olds are so dumb and we're always making up TikTok dances instead of reading books, but I just feel like we are so much more than that – *and* we know how to have fun! That's why I love our friendship, you know? We just really vibe – I'm chronically online because I'm busy reading all the comments under my posts and frantically responding to you – you're all so *funny*!'

She expertly talks them through using eyeliner to enhance their natural features, pointing out how it can change the shape of your face. She has to lean in close to the camera to do this, and is careful, making sure her hair hides the transparent tape pulling back the skin around her eyes and lifting her cheekbones.

'I don't have a monolid, but growing up I always wished I did so I could look more like my mom. All of you out there watching this with monolids, I want you to know you're beautiful, and I love you.' She blows them an exaggerated kiss, enjoying the way her nails catch the light.

A fan tells her, 'I wish I had your clear skin,' and accompanies her comment with several sobbing emojis.

'Honestly?' Sakura pauses as she moves from one brow to another. 'I just got really lucky that Yumi, my mom, has naturally good skin. I inherited it from her. Asian genes are THE best!'

She performs for her audience. She dips into her culture, telling them stories of trips to Tokyo, stacking up sushi plates at the conveyor belt restaurants, her favourite convenience store snacks that she stocks up on whenever she goes back, and the neighbourhood her mother grew up in. She is purposefully vague on details and timelines, vigilant, so she does not give away the fact that she's a decade older than they all think. As she instructs her audience on how to create a little heart on the inner corner of the eye with red eyeliner, Sakura recounts a moment from her childhood of bowing to her teachers when her family moved to Oregon and cringing with embarrassment when kids laughed at her. 'I think that was the first time I realised I was different, and felt like that was a bad thing.' She uses a pair of tweezers to stick a little silver gem in the middle of the heart and beams. '*Kawai!*'

She soaks up the praise like a flower in the sun, double-tapping a comment that reads: *You make me feel so much better about being half. Thank you.*

As she's finishing up, she spots a comment she'd missed a few minutes earlier: *This woman's name isn't Sakura, it's Amy.*

Sakura holds up two different shades of lipstick. The accusation makes her freeze for just a second too long. What – or, rather, who – the fuck is this?

'Blossoms, which one are we feeling?'

I went to school with her, I met her parents.

'"Sake Sweet" or "Meet Me in Shibuya"?' She rolls her eyes. 'These names are so *cringe.*'

She's NOT JAPANESE, GUYS, she's just a regular white girl from Oregon with white parents.

Sakura holds up a tiny mirror shaped like a salmon maki roll, and slowly applies the purple gloss to her lips. She takes her time, angling the mirror so it's all her audience can see. No one seems to have reacted so far, but a little distraction never hurts.

'OH, this?' she giggles when she spots the questions she was waiting for. 'Can you *believe* that this used to be my mom's when she was younger? I've fully taken it, she's not getting it back. I'm thinking of adding something similar to my store. What do you think? I could do all the different kinds of sushi!'

She used to act this way in high school too, even when people who actually WERE Japanese told her to stop. I really wish people would—

Sakura deletes the comments with a few quick swipes and smiles back into the camera, making a peace sign up against her cheek. This is the second time she's seen this username pull this shit, and it's one attempt too many. She recognises the name of the depressed, jealous bitch who always sat next to her in Geometry. A troll who was about to get blocked.

'*Mata ne!*' She sighs gently, pretending she'll miss them all. 'See you later! Until next time, friends!'

A Beautiful Lack of Consequence

Her mother is calling for her but she ignores it. She decides on a violent entrance – the saloon doors burst open, bang against the wall and swing back and forth behind her. As one, the men all swivel their heads her way. Even the bartender. Even the man sitting at the piano in the far corner, playing a little tune. She's wearing tight, high-waisted shorts, and a flannel shirt is loosely tied around her PIERCED/TATTOOED/FLAT navel. Her BLONDE/DARK/RED hair is long – too long – and tumbles down her back, shimmering as she sways. She's a pixelated stunner, of course, walks as if her hips are dislocated, jutting out to an extreme. Her breasts bounce and strain against the fabric. Her nipples peek through like little budding flowers. Totally fuckable. In a leather holster around her tiny waist is a BERETTA/SMITH&WESSON/GLOCK.

Stay vigilant, partner, these parts around here sure are dangerous.

The anticipation quickens her breath. She makes her way deeper into the room, her head turning first to the left, then to the right. The spurs on her cowboy boots clink as she moves. One hand rests casually on the BERETTA/SMITH &WESSON/GLOCK. As she reaches the bar, she tosses her BLONDE/DARK/RED hair over her shoulder and rests her breasts on the counter. From behind, she's a perfect figure eight and a wolf whistle whips around the room. She ignores it. One of the men finds himself at the bar too, standing next to her. His HANDLEBAR MOUSTACHE/CHIN STRAP/ SOUL PATCH moves when he speaks. A pistol (make and model unknown) is also holstered around his waist.

'Hey, beautiful,' the man says loudly and reaches out, slapping the bare skin of her ass cheek. The pianist stops his jaunty tune. She feels nothing.

You going to tolerate that kinda behaviour, partner?

There is no time to lose. She's been too slow to react before, and when that happens she has to start all over again. She spins around. Her breasts – with the nipples budding like little flowers – swing wildly. She immediately draws her BERETTA/SMITH&WESSON/ GLOCK – let's go with GLOCK – and pumps three rounds into the target's CHEST/STOMACH/ HEAD – let's go with HEAD. He dies straight away and his body fades as he hits the floor. No one moves. She is safe. Her purse fills with gold. She slips his drink calmly down her throat and sashays out of the saloon, already on the hunt for the next one.

Wow! You sure taught him a— PAUSE.

The girl, fourteen, whoops as she pulls off her headset. Her mother is calling her for dinner. She thunders down the stairs and a message flashes on the screen.

KEEP GOING?

KEEP GOING?

KEEP GOING?

Snow White

(EXTRACTS FROM *Stories to Tell Your Five-Year-Old*)

The free accommodation was handy, for sure, especially after I'd run away with literally nothing except the clothes on my back. But taking care of seven men? That lost its shine on day two, when I stepped into the downstairs bathroom to find yellow stains on the walls around the toilet seat like paintball splatters. Going near it made me gag. Contrary to what you've heard, I very much enjoyed my magical coma – or, as I thought of it at the time, my year off. It was profoundly irritating to be jolted out of bliss by a sweaty man whose crown slipped off his head and landed painfully on the bridge of my nose – it left a scar! Upon being rudely awoken by some 'prince', I punched him in the mouth for kissing me without my consent, stole his horse and fucked off.

Snow White. Just Snow White.
Don't you lump me in with those seven men.

Show a little bit of skin! Smile more!
Good girl.
Okay, well maybe not that much skin, that's a little too
much –
You're a little too much.

Fresh Meat

Four girls, four women, fresh meat, are sitting at the back of the lecture room waiting for the professor to arrive and launch them into *Political and Economic Theory 101*. They're young, intelligent and lustrous, the kind of women who lean towards each other when they speak, who hoover up knowledge and then diligently distribute it amongst themselves for future use. Listening to them, you'd be forgiven for thinking they do, in fact, know everything.

The entire room is alive with conversation and laughter, but today the four of them are unusually serious. Esperanza has brought the newspaper to the lecture because of the image on the front, and her agitation has infected them all.

'No one's talking about it,' Imani says, her eyes darting around the room. She's just come from her *Feminist Discourse Throughout History* module, where *everyone* had been talking about it. Her notes are punctuated with messy doodles and cartoon illustrations. On the page spread open in front of her, a small cow with purple markings stands under a crescent moon and chews the edge of the margin.

Biz is the one with the newspaper in her hands. Strands of her long, blow-dried hair obscure part of the headline.

The murder has been all over the news for days now, as protests rip through the country. Women marching with red paint drawn across their mouths, their hands shackled together. They've consumed the coverage endlessly, but the illustration of the young woman – just two years older than them, with her mouth taped shut and her brown eyes wide and wet – is new, and it has stirred up something in each of them. The worst part, which none of them have voiced aloud, is that she looks a lot like Suriya and Imani. She could have been their cousin.

'I'm sure some of them are talking about it,' Suriya says evenly. 'We're not the only ones in the room that care.'

Imani snorts. 'I don't think anyone here even knows her full name.' She wants to add, *because she's brown* but worries it will come out too blunt, upsetting her friends.

'They do. They have to,' Esperanza mutters, slumped forward on the desk. She's hungover, with the beginnings of a headache chewing at her temples and a longing for junk food, which she plans to hunt down straight after uni. 'She's everywhere.'

'How bad is it?' Suriya briefly massages Esperanza's head, making her sigh in relief.

'Mhhh. Want pizza.' She and Imani are the only ones in the group who drink, and she's starting to think Biz and Suriya have the right idea.

Four seats down, Imani – who drank at *least* as much as Esperanza did last night, but appears to have handled it much better – checks her eyeliner in her front-facing camera. 'We can get pizza afterwards? There's that place, like, ten minutes away which does a student discount if you eat before five.'

Esperanza nods into the table and they sit in silence for a minute, letting the chatter wash over them. Suriya flicks through some of the activists she follows online, wishing she had the means to jump on a plane and join them. 'I've heard there's a solidarity protest outside the embassy this weekend. We could go.'

No one says anything, but Biz finds her hand and squeezes hard.

'There's something I can't get out of my head,' Esperanza says. 'I'm sorry, because it's horrible. It's maybe the worst bit. But I can't stop thinking about what they . . . how they . . . her mouth.' She stops and swallows hard. 'I just can't stop thinking about the fact that whoever did this to her cut her tongue out and then gagged her, before she died.'

'It was before they killed her?'

'That's what the autopsy said. Her mouth was full of blood, so she had to have been alive.'

'Fuck. *Fuck*.' Suriya closes her eyes and rests her forehead on her fists. 'What the *fuck*.'

'It . . . well . . .' Esperanza sighs. 'It reminds me a bit of that punishment you were talking about the other day, Imani. From your feminism module.'

Imani frowns and leans forward to get a better view of Esperanza. 'The husband stitch?'

'Yes, that. I know it's not exactly the same, but there's something there, isn't there? It sounds batshit but I can't stop thinking that what happened to her is somehow connected to what was done to those women centuries ago. There are these parallels. These horrific parallels.'

'Urgh!' Biz groans. She glances at Imani, who's already flipping through her notes. 'Are we – are *you* – really going to intellectualise *this*, Esperanza?' Even as she says it, Biz knows the others won't see it the way she does; the extra distance that Esperanza gets to enjoy from this gruesome murder because she's European and white. *Intellectualise the dead white girls*, she wants to say, *and let us grieve her in peace.*

But Esperanza has a slightly frantic energy today, and Biz knows her friend has also lived through a violence none of them have, one that she carries with her still, so she doesn't push it further. Even Suriya, who usually stays out of the heavy debates, is paying attention now. The moment goes unaddressed.

Imani is shaking her head. 'Are you saying there's a direct correlation? Because if you are, you're not making sense. Husband stitching was a European phenomenon, there's no evidence of it going over to Asia.'

'It's more like a symbolic connection, I think,' Esperanza says, her dark eyes sincere. 'This kind of sexual violence through mutilation and murder. A spiritual silencing.'

For a moment, no one knows how to respond. Esperanza has always been a little kooky, though usually not with such a sensitive topic. But Imani suddenly lurches forward with interest. 'I think I see what you mean, actually.'

'Me too!' Suriya says. 'I mean, I don't know anything about husband stitching but in my international law seminars we talk about the psychological destruction that comes with mass violence, and whether or not that constitutes – or should constitute – genocide.'

Biz sighs and resists the urge to roll her eyes. 'Remind me what it is again?' She traces the outline of her lips with two fingers in anticipation.

'This fucked-up thing they did to women who transgressed in some way, like, four hundred years ago. Apparently, it was a common punishment for adultery. They'd hold the woman down and literally stitch her mouth shut by sewing an X across her lips – or it could be in the shape of a cross – and only her husband or father was allowed to cut the strings for her to eat.'

'Or fuck,' Suriya adds, the words coming out rough and loud. The hoops in her ears reflect a creamy gold on to her skin. Esperanza folds her arms over the desk and buries her face into it with a soft exhale. Imani reaches out to gently tug a ballpoint pen from Suriya's hands, adding '*or fuck*' in the margin of her notes.

Biz has stopped tracing her lips and instead presses her fingers to them hard, her mouth bleaching white. 'There's, like, documentation of that?'

'Some. Not loads. Do you know the story of Lyssa?'

'No.'

'She – or it – was supposedly this fire-breathing monster who lived in a cave overlooking the Mediterranean, and she'd attack sailors and villagers and eat them.'

'Right . . .'

'Well, before she became a monster she was a girl from one of the villages with a beautiful voice. Eventually her singing drove the men so wild they couldn't bear to hear it any more, so they held her down and sewed her mouth shut.'

'A spiritual silencing,' Esperanza interjects, and Suriya frowns at the back of her head. 'Um, Es, I think the physical assault is more the point here? It's sexual violence.'

'Of course there's no doubt about it – but why go to all that effort? It's *more* than sexual violence. It's a psychological attack, not just towards her but to all other women. A warning. Symbolically speaking, what does it mean to literally remove a woman's ability to speak?'

Although she tries her best, Biz cannot keep the incredulity out of her voice. 'That's your evidence that the husband stitch was a thing? A *myth*?'

'There's other evidence too!' Imani says defensively. 'And, not to get all *Beginner's Guide to History* on you, but mythology is often a reflection of fears and morals of the people it's about – or who wrote it. Lyssa was probably some poor girl who did nothing wrong and got absolutely tormented anyway.'

'You know Lyssa was a Greek goddess of uncontrollable rage and madness?' Esperanza's voice is muffled from her squashed face. 'I can really relate.'

They say nothing for a moment. Biz gestures to Esperanza and glances over at Imani questioningly. Asking, without asking.

'Big fight with pretzel boy last night,' Imani mouths, watching her friend carefully in case she looks up. 'I think they're done.'

The women had a rule that the people they dated only got called by their real names when they had made it to the three-month mark. Pretzel boy had barely lasted three weeks, but they had all noticed how much Esperanza glowed around him.

Shit, Biz grimaces and Suriya reaches over to stroke Esperanza's head again, changing the subject.

'You know the husband stitch means something different now, right?'

'Yeah yeah, I know, Suri. The extra stitch doctors sometimes give women to keep it tight after they give birth. But we only have anecdotal evidence of that too, right? So it can't be real, right, Biz?' Imani's so tense she's fiddling with the fraying edge of her headscarf, pulling the fabric further apart. A bang from the front of the room makes the four of them jump and a loud cheer rises from the crowd as a student whoops, having successfully lobbed a full can of Coke into the recycling bin several metres away from his seat.

'Fuck's sake,' Esperanza moans into the table.

'Look . . . I just don't buy the claim that it was going on all over the place. Especially if you only have a fairy tale to go off on. And the impracticality of it.' Biz glances towards the door in search of their professor. He's over ten minutes late at this point, and she's irritated. Thousands and thousands of pounds in debt for a handful of hours a week and professors who won't let last-minute students into their lectures but seem to have no problem with turning up late themselves. *I turned down a shift for this.* She directs her frustration towards her friends instead.

'There are much easier ways to torture women than to stitch their mouths shut. And anyway – what does this have to do with *her*?' She slides the newspaper roughly back towards Esperanza, forcing her head up. Anger wells up in her throat. 'Why are we talking about this?'

They look towards Esperanza, who sits up abruptly and flushes. 'Well, it was either that or we go back to sitting in silence! I'm just trying to distract us!'

'But you're making no sense! Why would you bring up violence from the past to distract us from the violence of the present?' Biz says, at the same time as Suriya says, more gently, 'I'm not sure we should be distracted from it, actually.'

They all stare at each other for a moment, then Esperanza rests her elbows on the table again, muttering, 'I'd rather debate something from the past than talk about how powerless and scared I feel. How this shit worms its way into every good thing in our lives, even our friendships, and makes it heavy and corrosive.'

In the days since the news broke, Esperanza has found herself obsessing about the mutilated, murdered girl, and it both enrages and terrifies her. She thinks about what the woman's final moments might have been like, over and over. The confusion and pain and terror; the fact that her body was thrown out of a moving train and left by the side of a road, the hundreds of thousands of women who felt her death so viscerally they were pouring into the streets, risking their own lives to avenge her, and voice their own pain and rage and disbelief. Esperanza thinks about the best day of her life which then became the worst night of her life, and how she jokes about it and dissects it and cries about it and writes about it and obsesses over it, and how all of that didn't matter, in the end, when she tried to report it. And the world didn't stop, when she needed it to.

Most of all, she cannot stop thinking about the fact that after all that, after all the protesting and risk and pain, the world would move on and more women would die, and nothing would change. She cannot bear this. It makes her want to fight everyone, even her closest friends.

Suriya nudges her. 'Why don't you come with me to the embassy protest this weekend?' she says, as Biz pulls out a box of dates from her backpack and offers it to them all.

'I've stuffed them with walnuts.' She makes sure to catch Esperanza's eye and smiles. 'Sorry for snapping at you, babe. I'm upset today. Pizza will— Oh, at fucking last!'

Waving apologetically, the lecturer arrives and starts to fiddle with the projector. The chatter around the women grows louder, and the change of pace helps some of the tension between them dissipate, like a deflating balloon. Imani hooks her chin on to her friend's shoulder. 'Would you describe our friendship as heavy and corrosive?' she murmurs, and Biz laughs loudly, relaxing back into her seat.

Biz and Imani have known each other since primary school. Calm, stoic Suriya is Imani's cousin, who welcomed Esperanza with open arms when she joined their trio. Esperanza met Imani at an abortion rights protest in Berlin, when they were both on their gap year. She'd stumbled into the protest entirely by accident, lost the group of women she'd been with and then spotted Imani looking incredibly cool with her megaphone and sunglasses, in the middle of January. Esperanza knows her friend is the backbone of their group, the clever one, the peacemaker. She stares into Imani's earnest brown eyes, so dark they're almost black, and thinks about how she stood with her in the smoking area for more than an hour last night, picking over the argument she'd had with Aurelio. She'd been a perfect friend, furious and indignant on Esperanza's behalf and insisting Aurelio had just made the biggest mistake of his life. And this morning, she'd simply kissed Esperanza's cheek and handed her a flat white and a warm pain au chocolat without saying a word. Imani has always been good at digesting sadness, a habit she picked up from her wary, weary parents, whose jarring experiences emigrating to Europe had never quite faded from the way they carried themselves. Sometimes, Imani jokes that her heart is made of quicksand.

Esperanza, on the other hand, has never been taught to expect the worst. She's so angry she wants to flip the table over and scream until all the people in the room stop talking and start screaming with her, smashing windows and destroying things and setting cars on fire. She wants them all to riot and stun the world into action, instead of sitting in a meaningless class, feeling sick and knowing that soon there will be another woman's name and face in the headlines.

She looks away from Imani and slaps her hand down on the image of the dead woman; the bloodied tape obscuring her mouth. Her entire face has become a crime scene, and Esperanza hates it.

'I don't know how we're supposed to live this way.' Her voice grows louder. 'I don't know how I'm going to be able to sit here and listen to this man talk about neo-classical economics, or whatever this one's on, knowing that this – that she – is our reality.'

At this, the two women sitting in the row in front of them briefly glance up at her, looking bemused. As they turn back, one of them says, 'I actually quite like neo-classical economics.'

'That's because your parents are rich,' her friend replies, and Esperanza feels her anger drain and pool around her feet. She's suddenly exhausted.

The lecture theatre darkens and a sea of laptop screens dot the lecture hall. Suriya thinks she hears her friend let out a sob, and tries to find her hand in the gloom.

'It just feels like the world keeps finding newer, more creative ways to brutalise us.'

'RIGHT,' the lecturer shouts, 'let's get going then,

shall we? Apologies for being a little late today.' Appearing on the projection screen behind him are the words: *Fallacies of contemporary austerity policies: Britain, emergency budgets, and the politics of recession.*

Biz groans. 'I'm on the edge of my fucking seat.'

Reflections

The mirror's bottom third is stained with water-marks. A line of mould, a decade old, runs along the silicone keeping the mirror glued to the wall. The door? Poorly balanced – it flies open and crashes against the tile even when lightly pushed. A grey dent from the metal handle.

A girl stuffs toilet paper into her knickers to cover up the maroon stain. She glances at herself while pumping the soap dispenser. No lunch today, either. Tears in her eyes, she asks, *why me?* She hears the tannoy announce her train's arrival. Rushes out with her eyes and hands still wet. Soap suds on the handle. Forgets to close the tap. Ten minutes pass, and the water runs and runs.

Then: a grandmother applies lipstick carefully, very carefully. She saw a mother clutching a small boy on the platform, wonders if he'll need to come in here while they wait. Wipes the corners of her mouth and checks her teeth. Stretches the skin on her face and wonders if she'll ever stop pulling. Yearning.

Still for a little while. After school, a boy leans in real close. Breath fogs up the glass; he examines the purpling of his eye. That will swell shut soon, he knows. He hides in there for a long time. Not hides, sorry, *waits*. He waits in there for a long, long time. Leaves quietly; the door does not bang.

The next person tilts their head to the left, looking at the angular sharpness of their jaw. On the good days the jaw is good, on the bad days the jaw is a disaster. *Would it – should I – is it –* they stop. One day, maybe, everything will be softer. There's a bouquet of purple flowers propped up between mirror and sink. Gift. Carried them all day, considers leaving them here for the next person. Picks them back up. They leave; a queue is forming. No one says anything, and they're pleased. They feel relieved, and then they feel angry about their relief. The small triumph curdles.

Air? Stale. Her shift is done. A woman places her shopping bag down on the grimy floor. Stares at herself like a haunted thing. Her hands spread like two starfish across her belly, still hers. Thinks, *what the fuck will I do now?* Imagines she's on a surgeon's table, a laser passing over her body. Getting rid of it cleanly, painlessly, no evidence. No waiting. She wishes that's how it worked. Doesn't know who to tell – *if* to tell. Ignores the first train, and then the second. Someone knocks, makes her jump. Her scarf swings on its metal hook on the back of the door. Slash of red.

Creeping darkness. The last train comes in seventeen minutes; she must lock the door behind her. Exhausted woman. Brings her sprays, her cloth, her miniature stepladder. Registers herself briefly – brown skin, deep eyes, black hair. Her lower back aches and aches and aches.

The stains on the bottom third of the mirror never seem to go, not even with vinegar. The small room stinks of shit and vinegar. Piss and vinegar. Bleach. She lifts the flap of her yellow glove, checks her watch. There is no time for looking: she has wreckage to clean.

Lilith

(EXTRACTS FROM *Stories to Tell Your Five-Year-Old*)

Oh, sweet, patient Eve. I don't know how she bore it for as long as she did. I was out of there before the sun set. How disappointing, to have existed for a matter of hours, and immediately be harassed. I wanted *everything*, all at once. I pressed my face into the sweet, damp earth in delight, I shivered at the feel of water, and how it eluded my grip. I almost cried at the stringy bitterness of the leaves I shoved into my mouth. He should have joined me, instead of attempting to *assert*, to *dominate*, to *control*. It's not that I wasn't tempted to do that too; of course I was. But it was much more pleasurable to marvel at the way sand coats the skin like a fine powder, or press a finger to the thorn of a rose and watch a little drop of blood appear. Metallic on the tongue.

Adam wanted me to lie silently beneath him as he exerted control over my body. The idea was repulsive, flattening, like I was a dead thing, without any desire of my own. He didn't get what he wanted, and though it stung at first, I'm not particularly fussed about my womb turning into a graveyard. I never wanted to give my body to anyone except myself, anyway.

The Witch Queen, Lilith

Blood-ridden, with Little Use for Vocal Cords

She was born fierce, with a pair of wings, but the problem was that they would not, could not, pull her out of there. And then she made the terrible mistake of being unhappy. So somewhere along the way, she sold her wings. She traded them for vocal cords so she could sing, and managed to string together notes as mesmerising and light-filled as the glass beads the women looped around their necks. No one knew it, but she sang the sun into the sky in the mornings and charmed it into strengthening the crops. The women would pick the grapes and harvest the olives and sell the best oil and wine in the land in thick terracotta jars decorated with patterns that looked like jagged teeth. The town flourished. And for a while, she was happier.

Alas.

The village men accused her of being too pleased with herself, too loose, of enjoying the breeze on her skin just a little too much. They held her down and sewed her mouth shut one sticky morning, limbs rope-tied, her skin torn up from the struggle. And the women saw the warning and would not look at her or offer their hand when she lay there in cold shock. So, blood-ridden, and with little use for vocal cords, she bartered them for gills, hoping to dive deeper into colder, murkier waters. She found, to her sanguine delight, that she could see and breathe much better down there, in the clear waters of the Aegean, and so she started digging up pearls that were fatter and more luminescent than everybody else's. She worked so very hard that salt crystals formed along her stitches. A pull in the base of her stomach began telling her she just hadn't quite been ready for the places her wings could take her to, before. So she set up a stall under a dove tree and started selling the pearls, with the intention of buying back her wings. She seemed to bloom, with the birds spreading their wings and singing so alluringly that the air around her trembled. The women of the land bought up her pearls to string in their hair so they could gleam under the sun, and word spread of their lustre. For a while, she was happier.

Alas.

The oyster-shuckers of the village became angered by the ethereal quality of her pearls, outshining the rest, and one day they surrounded her and sliced her gills off with their sea-daggers, the salt burning the wounds, and she could not even cry for help. They threw the gills, now browning and withered, back at her feet. The women, afraid of the tainting, ground the pearls she had delivered into powder and sprinkled them back into the sea. She had little choice but to trade her useless gills for something else. The question was, what now? It took longer this time, and she grew emaciated and embittered. Eventually, she traded her gills for a set of teeth. Not the kind of teeth you and I eat with – no, no, something far more sinister.

This is how she did it: she slaughtered a lamb. She took her withered, dead gills and removed the lamb's intestines and fried them both together with wild garlic and aconite, until they were fragrant and tender. She carried the dish to the mountains, hid herself, and waited. In this regard, she was lucky. The first beast that came along was an enormous brown bear. Its ochre eyes fastened on the food within seconds, and when the poison had taken effect, she cut the bear's teeth from its maw. She left its majestic body for the wolves, and washed the teeth in the sea to make them her own. They looked like stalactites adorning the mouth of a cave: very beautiful, yes, but quick to lacerate. She stole a sea-dagger from those oyster-shuckers, retreated to the cave in the mountains overlooking the village, and sliced the rusting threads muzzling her mouth shut. She felt the beads of blood well up from the punctures dotting her lips and let her tongue savour the taste. The process of inserting these teeth was unbelievably easy. Her jaw stretched wide to accept them. There was no pain; even the holes ripped into her mouth flesh stopped their dripping.

And for a while, she was . . . not happier per se, but no longer grieving. She pulled fish from the waves and ate them right there and then like a wild thing. She drank the salt from the sea like it could douse her bitterness – but it was not enough. She began to get hungrier and hungrier. Slowly, anger lodged in her gut like a fishbone and set the lining of her stomach on fire. It started to send smoke up her throat; at night she struggled to breathe from the heat. She watched the village heave and stretch beneath her like molasses, and her teeth strained forward in yearning. As if leashed. As if the leash decayed and frayed with every pull. She was so very hungry. In the dying daylight she watched the gulls circle overhead and could not sing with them or dive with them or fly with them. She was born fierce, with a pair of wings, but somewhere along the way she sold them. The problem was that they would not, could not, pull her out of there. So she bares her teeth at the sky, her roars turned inward. The smoke pours out of her throat.

God, you're easily offended, aren't you?

Woman on the Internet

'Good morning, Mom.' Her daughter's voice materialised in her right ear. Despite herself, Shay smiled.

'Hiya, Linny.'

'Whose file am I pulling today?'

'Number 000340, username: alphacocksucker1488.' The four monitors blinked into life as Shay pulled the goggles over her eyes, thrusting her chin forward to adjust the silicone edging on her cheekbones.

'On it, Mom.'

No one at work had been surprised when she'd been fired from the force after refusing to take the mandatory compassionate leave. Twenty-five years of service in the Special Weapons Unit cut short because of a silly little breakdown. Shay had been furious about it at first, but once she'd realised she no longer needed her job to fulfil her mission, it had barely mattered. And they'd been generous about it and let her go with a decent severance package. Combined with her pension, it had been enough to keep the gravestone clean and well looked-after, and the whole operation ticking along nicely.

'I've got him, Mom. Twenty-eight, unmarried, works in insurance. Several priors from your list. Armed. Resides in . . . Knoxville.'

'That's the one. I want you monitoring his chatter please, I'm going to set up Op Z. It's going to take a while. I want to know immediately if he comes online.'

'*Online* online?'

'No, just any virtual comms.'

'On it, Mom.'

They worked in silence, Shay's breath slowing to a steady rate as she carefully, methodically, ran through her code on her top-left monitor – double- and then triple-checking it. Z, for Zoloft. She'd thought about calling it 'Linny's Revenge', but then the chances of it being traced back to her increased. And Shay did not intend to be stopped, especially not because of an irrational decision.

'Hey . . . Mom?' Linny asked, carefully.

'Yep?'

'Did you have a good day today?'

She hesitated for a long moment, her eyes flickering between the monitors. 'Remember what I said about casual conversation. We keep it professional, okay?'

'Right.' Linny sounded embarrassed. 'Sorry. I'll let you know when there's an update.'

Shay suppressed a yawn. She should have been alert, ready for battle, but lately her body had been betraying her mind. These days, she rose late – maybe eleven, or even noon. Artificial lights, painkillers, stretches, one shower a day. Perhaps every other day. Her skin, once a glowing olive-brown, was now dull and tinged with yellow, as were the whites of her eyes. Her new apartment had blank walls, her discount furniture was either black or a sludgy grey. Grey clothes too. She occasionally glanced at herself in the bathroom mirror, expecting atrophy and decay, but was surprised each time, in a detached kind of way, that this lifestyle somewhat suited her. It had been too easy to retreat entirely from her life offline once she left the military world.

Linny crackled back to life. 'He's at work. Been messaging a lot – there's a girl he wants to date.'

'He's texting her?'

'Not right now. She asked him to give her space after their date last night, he's real mad about it.'

'So who's he talking to?'

'A buddy, I'm assuming. They're calling her a "Stacy", joking about spiking her and forcing her to—'

'We've got plenty of data on that already. I want to know who he's talking to, if we've got him on file. Can you check?'

'I've done background on him – assuming he's a "him" – already. Nothing in our system.'

Shay frowned. She was certain they had every one of the targets in Knoxville pinpointed.

'Is the buddy local?'

Silence as Linny flicked through their text history, before announcing, 'Negative. I think he's a coaster.'

'Regional?'

'Not even the same country. He's either in Colombia – the country – or British Columbia, Canada, but I'm going to say Canada, based on the colloquialisms and speech pattern.'

'Canada's in our range. Open a file on him. 000482.'

'On it, Mom.'

It had been easy. Too easy. She had stripped back her entire life and dedicated it instead to the best form of satisfaction she could think of, nice and violent, but impossible to trace. They sat in front of her: tiny strips of blue dissolvable paper, protected only by a small plastic matchbox with PROPERTY OF THE UNITED STATES MILITARY stamped on to it. Shay was careful never to let her skin come into contact with them. Just possessing these was enough to land her in a maximum security cell for the rest of her life, but it was astounding how invisible grief can make a person, and she'd walked out with several of the matchboxes wedged into the sole of her shoe the day they let her go. Enough to kill thousands. She sometimes liked to imagine the looks on her former colleagues' faces if she were ever to get caught. They'd be impressed, despite themselves. She knew it.

Even Samuel hadn't known the true intention of the decades-long operation she'd spearheaded, only ever being told small snippets of information.

'We've got residue down to 0.01 per cent,' she'd told him one night, as she spoon-fed rice and peas into their eighteen-month-old's mouth, 'but there's a couple of Quantico bolos who reckon their tests could pick something up.'

'That's terrific,' Samuel had responded – and Shay had known he really meant it. 'Just 0.01 per cent? A perfect way to kill.'

'The body just shuts itself down. We could make it a paralytic' – Shay had kissed the top of Linny's fluffy-duckling head – 'or agonisingly painful. It's attacking the brain, after all. But that 0.01 per cent. I'm not happy with it.'

'That's practically untraceable.'

'It's still too much. This is going to be a cornerstone of our *foreign policy*. We'll have to get it to 100 per cent. Somehow.'

Samuel, then still in awe of her, had smiled. 'Attagirl.'

Now, she wondered if he'd still be so proud. All the money her ex-husband had left her, when he left her, had gone into this corner of her apartment. Her playground hummed and glowed soothingly, the way only well-maintained, high-quality tech can.

There were four different monitors, the desk – one of the few genuine mahogany pieces around these days – and the server, encased in grey acrylic, emitting enough heat to warm her entire home. The chair (memory foam, automatic massager, expensive) was designed especially for her body. Many nights, she slept in it.

'Op Z is loaded. Can you bring up the target's comms, please?'

Even though she didn't need to, Shay spent the next several hours watching the target's messages flicker back and forth, with her eyes narrowed. Everything would be logged by Linny, so she was at her leisure to flick through the jokes about raping women, the whining about how hard his life was, even the constant harassment of the poor girl he'd met recently. He sent her a hologram of a kitten with drooping whiskers. When she opened it, the kitten screamed at her in a cartoonish, high voice, 'You've really hurt my feelings. I thought you were different.'

The girl didn't respond, and it made Shay smile.

It had been four days since she'd figured out the code that could *finally* get Linny involved properly; the stakes felt higher, the work more urgent. Shay had forced herself to plan and practise – if she rushed, she could fuck everything up. It took all her willpower to eat, stretch and shower that morning before she took a seat at the mahogany desk and began compulsively running her hands on the underside of the wood to check for splinters. Shay was ambidextrous, giving her an advantage in the field; she operated a controller with her right hand and had built a specialised mouse into the lining of a black glove, which she wore on her left.

She forced herself to take ten slow, deep breaths. There was an exercise Samuel had taught her, a few months after they'd both passed basic training and were attempting to enter the special weapons programme. The stress had made her jumpy and impulsive. 'You block one nostril,' he'd said, 'take a deep breath in, then block the other nostril, release the first one, and breathe out. Repeat.'

He'd make her do it ten times, and then he would say some shit like, 'Now picture your loved ones smiling at you, telling you they love you.' Or, 'Imagine you're sitting under a waterfall and letting it wash away your fear.' Shay could never stomach that nonsense, until she'd started on this mission. Now, as she breathed, she thought of her target. *The* target, the one she'd been

tracking for months. Her fingers were itching to elimin-
ate him, to hear the sudden suck of air as a final breath
was pulled from his lungs.

Everything had to be perfect. Shay had done this
at least a hundred times by now, but tonight felt like
her first time all over again. He was the reason she had
betrayed her country, imploded her life and unleashed
a world-changing weapon upon the world. Shay had no
doubt that she would eventually be caught, her methods
discovered, and then everyone would know about the
ticking time bomb she had released on to the internet.
A brand-new way to kill.

Also on her desk was an empty pill bottle – *the* empty
pill bottle – of antidepressants with her ex-husband's
name on them. A reminder, for the days she felt too
numb, her limbs slow and stiff. Once, before Linny
burst into their lives, they'd sat on the floor of their old
house and watched a documentary about the thousands
of kamikaze pilots who'd flown their planes into Allied
ships during World War II, killing themselves and as
many servicemen as they could. Two hours of grainy
footage and black-and-white photos of Japanese pilots
had left Shay in awe and Samuel in tears. Afterwards,
they'd lain in bed in their favourite position: curled up
butt-to-butt, soles of their feet touching. Samuel had
told her about his mother's family history and her great-
great-uncle who'd been one of those pilots, and the
ripple effects his death had had on their family. It was
one of the few times her then-husband spoke about
his heritage. 'Kamikaze means "divine wind",' he'd

explained, 'from this story in Japanese history about an enemy fleet whose boats were diverted or destroyed by winds sent from the gods. The kamikaze pilots were mostly young, in their early twenties, and you were supposed to volunteer to do it. But so many of them were forced into it, knowing they'd be executed if they didn't.' Here, Samuel's voice had trembled. 'Would you have been able to do it? I don't know if I could.' Shay had turned to hug him, blinking away her own tears. This was back in the better days, when she could cry and laugh as easily as she could breathe. She'd never answered him, but they both knew she would have said yes.

These days Shay forced herself to think of those men on the rare occasions she tried to talk herself out of her mission. The one she'd set herself the day after she walked into her home on the military base, pulling off her dust-flecked mask to find her daughter convulsing and twitching on the floor like a poisoned rat. Grey foam and vomit crusted her mouth; the bottle empty and slippery in her sweaty hand. Samuel's antidepressants.

'You've been quiet for a long time. Is there anything I can help with, Mom?' Shay knew this was an automatic prompt from Linny, a feature she'd programmed for the moments when she got too sucked into the past. But the question still tore at her a little bit.

It had been hard to log off when Shay had first programmed the system's built-in assistant to replicate her daughter's voice, speech patterns and personality. The software was impressive, AI designed to probe every possible answer to a question and mine for information.

Within weeks, Shay was having the kinds of conversations with Linny that she'd always dreamed of: about school, about Samuel, and about her work, which Linny was desperate to understand.

One evening, though, Linny, laughing at Shay's joke – something mundane about online dating – had sighed and said, 'I wonder when I'll go on *my* first date.' It was like someone had picked Shay's body up and flung it down on to the floor, knocking all the air from her. She'd ripped off her headset and vomited down herself as she struggled to pull the goggles off her face. She reset Linny immediately. Her data was wiped, and Shay set firmer boundaries with Linny 2.0. The last thing she would allow herself to do was crumble before she could avenge her daughter. She was the judge, jury and executioner; there would be no room for weakness.

Shay's gloved hand twitched in anticipation, the matchbox filled with tiny blue slivers just inches away. She knew she might have to wait for several more hours, but her entire body was tense; a coiled snake waiting to be stepped upon.

At 21:30 hours, the target slouched on to his bed and pulled his laptop open. His face filled her bottom-left monitor, and Shay took a sharp breath in as she scanned his features. He looked like a perfectly average man. Balding slightly, black-rimmed glasses, pale with dark circles under his eyes, nondescript. He could be anyone. For a moment, they seemed to lock eyes and stare directly at each other, before his eyes flicked back to the screen.

'Linny, do a perimeter sweep and make sure we're still incognito,' Shay whispered, even though she knew there was no way he could see or hear her. But this was too important to mess up.

The moment Linny confirmed their security was intact, Shay checked on the other inhabitants of the target's apartment. Both men, both in their rooms, unlikely to come looking. One seemed acceptable – or, at least, Linny had found no evidence that he harassed and attacked women online – although he was frustratingly indifferent to the beliefs of his room-mate. The other was a nightmare, almost as dangerous as her target. He, too, was on Shay's list.

Installing the spyware had been easy. So was invading the privacy of strangers. The next step would be easier still, especially for a woman like her.

'I'm ready when you are, Mom,' her daughter whispered in her ear. This was Linny's favourite part.

'All right,' Shay murmured, 'let's freeze alphacocksucker's functionality in T minus two. I want your eyes on both civvies. One's already got his hand down his pants, so let's keep that going for the next couple of hours at least.'

Linny sounded excited. 'I've queued up his hardcore favourites, Mom, he won't be taking his eyes off his phone for a while.'

'Good. The other one's working with headphones on. That's okay, but he usually goes to the kitchen around twenty-three hundred hours, so I want you to distract him with a mild software malfunction. Something easy to motivate him to fix it – your last attempt was too aggressive.'

'On it, Mom. T minus forty-five seconds.'

Shay took a breath and exhaled slowly. She flexed her gloved hand a couple of times, then carefully opened the plastic matchbox, exposing the pale blue sheets.

'Go.'

Linny seized control of the target's laptop as Shay finally ran the code she'd spent years perfecting. Her movements were steady and deliberate, her breath even. Only a slight twitch in her right foot gave her away.

In front of her, the target sat up in bed, swearing at the screen and trying to shut the entire machine down. It wouldn't work.

Shay's top-left monitor beeped softly, flashing green. Moving quickly now, she took her gloved hand and pressed it down on the stack of pale blue squares open before her. One sheet, or it could have been two, stuck delicately to the tip of her finger.

Shay curled her hand into a fist, ensuring the sheet was safely tucked into her palm, and turned her attention to the fourth, most dangerous monitor on the far right, positioned next to the others on her desk. This screen was unique. It was made of a viscous material that shimmered like pinkish, liquified pearls. Perks of her old job. She'd committed treason to secure it.

'Passage is clear, Mom. Your mic's hot.'

'Hello, alphacocksucker1488,' Shay said quietly. The man froze with a jolt, his eyes flitting up to his laptop's built-in camera. He inhaled sharply.

'What the fuck . . . Who is this?'

Squeezing the blue sliver tightly in her palm, she sat up and braced herself against the floor, squeezing the backs of her thighs against the leather chair. The fourth monitor began to flash rapidly. *Grey-white-grey-white-grey-white-white-white-white.* Now or never.

'I'm here to rectify something,' she said, before punching through the monitor with as much strength as she could muster. Her body exploded forwards and pain erupted through her entire arm – like her veins had hardened and calcified – as it was swallowed into the pearly screen. The target yelped in shock as Shay's fist burst through his own screen, punching a hole straight through his Skybook and sending fibreglass shards spraying across the bed. Before he could react, Shay had grabbed his collar and slapped the poisonous patch on to his neck, ensuring it was securely attached before she whipped her hand back through the void and cradled it to her chest as the man hundreds of miles away from her stiffened and fell back on to the bed, unable to move. He hadn't even had time to cry out. The monitor returned to its pink hue.

Shay gave herself a minute, slowly peeling off the glove through gritted teeth. The process of bringing digital violence to life felt like plunging her hand into a deep-fat fryer. The pain was the one thing the Special Weapons Unit had never managed to fix; the main reason they'd never exploited the potential of this weapon any further. Under her orders, all prototypes had been destroyed. All but one.

'Alphacocksucker1488 is tagged, Mom!' Linny announced breathily, her voice betraying her excitement. 'The drug is taking effect now. Based on his body weight and height, hearing loss will occur at zero one fifteen. Vision at zero one forty, tops.'

'Roger that. Angle his camera so I can see him better and commence Op Z.'

The target's Skybook was disabled but still functional, which was important for the plan to work. The technology that she'd stolen once she'd been honourably discharged was marvellous, a weapon that would have revolutionised her country's intelligence gathering, had it not caused agony to the operator. Shay had killed close to a hundred of these men with her gloved hand, her poison, her pearly screen, but she'd never had the chance to involve her daughter the way she would tonight.

'Patch is secure and his vitals are on display. Op Z is live in three . . . two . . . one.'

Shay held her breath as she watched her daughter's beautiful face form in front of her. A perfect holographic rendition of her high cheekbones and hazel, upturned eyes. It even captured the way Linny used to frown and purse her lips when she was concentrating. Shay felt her face grow hot and forced the tears back down, pinching the skin of her stomach painfully with one hand. It was all she could do not to touch her daughter's cheek.

The target could see her daughter too, projected from the final remnants of his useless Skybook screen.

Her eyes were narrowed and focused on him. He was motionless, able only to blink and breathe, as his chest rose and fell rapidly. His eyes were open in a silent scream. The men often soiled themselves when the paralytic took hold, but this one hadn't, to Shay's surprise.

'Wow! I look *so* cool, Mom!' Linny whispered enthusiastically. 'You've done an amazing job with this new coding. I'm gonna start now.'

Shay nodded and made herself sit back. It was her daughter's time to shine. The hologram shimmered as Linny started speaking.

'I'm sure you're confused by what's just happened, so let me help you out. I've paralysed you to ensure I have your full attention – but don't worry. It's temporary! You won't stay this way.' The hologram paused and showed him all angles of her face.

'Remember me? You and your sick, depraved little friends targeted and harassed me for months. Remember why? Nod your head if you do!' Linny pouted. 'Guess not, huh? My name is Linny Melrose-Sasaki. Ringing any bells? I'm the CHILD whose video on fourth-wave feminism went viral, and you really hated it. In the video I talked about the cyber violence young women face, and the ways in which our technology was enabling it, and you got *really* mad about that. In fact, you were so adamant that I was wrong, you proceeded to violently attack me. You drove me off the internet for a while. I was fourteen, and I was really, really smart. Smarter than you.'

The hologram of her daughter stuck her tongue out, and Shay's eyes flickered over to the top-left monitor, checking the target's vitals. One hundred and twenty beats per minute.

'It was like being in a *war.* You were relentless,' Linny continued. 'You posted my address online and encouraged people to come find me. You personally told me how much you fantasised about raping me at gunpoint and then shooting me in the head.'

One hundred and twenty-four.

Linny grinned. 'You went on and on and *on* about how much you hated me. But not just me! It wasn't personal, right? You hate all women. You think we owe you our bodies, that we're inferior to you in every way and that we're shallow and vapid, only picking conventionally good-looking men to sleep with instead of the nice guys like you. Aw.' She pouted again, playfully. 'So sad!'

One hundred and twenty-seven.

'T minus two hours and forty-five. You're doing great, honey,' Shay breathed.

'I researched you, after you attacked me online and drove me to swallow my dad's pills. I counted up all the messages that you personally sent me – shall we play a game?'

Alphacocksucker's eyeballs bulged. Shay could see the tears forming as he remained unable to blink.

'How many times did you call me "cancerous"? Any guesses? Seventy-four. How many times did you threaten to rape and kill me? Three hundred and three. How many times did you tell me to kill myself? One hundred and seventeen. How many times did you promise me you were going to shoot me while I was at school? Thirty-one.' Linny's voice rose as she spoke, and by the end, she was shouting.

'HOW MANY TIMES DID YOU SEND ME VIDEOS OF YOUNG GIRLS BEING VIOLENTLY RAPED, WITH MY FACE SUPERIMPOSED ON TO THEM? HOW MANY? NINETY-EIGHT TIMES, YOU PIECE OF SHIT.'

Alphacocksucker had tears running freely down his face now, and Shay wished she still owned a phone, to capture the glorious sight.

'I decided to learn everything about men like you, who hunt women online and think the world is to blame for your loneliness, and hunt *you* all down one by one. No one else seemed to be bothered enough to stop evil men like you, despite the mass shootings, the racism, and the neo-Nazism. "1488" – you think I don't know what your little dogwhistle means? I know everything about you, alphacocksucker. I infiltrated your forums, read your whiny posts about how straight, white men like you are so hard done by, how no one will fuck you even though you're *a really good guy*, and how women's rights have destroyed society. You're boringly predictable. I know what you're planning to do to that girl you're messaging. I know you're going to tell her it's all her fault afterwards, that she deserved it. Hate to break it to you, buddy, but you're not touching her. Or any other woman, ever again.'

One hundred and forty.

'I know some of your friends are in government.'

Linny had stopped smiling, her three-dimensional mouth now curled in disgust. 'I know you people are everywhere. You're lawyers, soldiers, teachers, bartenders, labourers, bankers. You use codes and military tactics and act like you've got a little army going, don't you? I'm right, aren't I? Blink if I'm right, baby!'

One hundred and forty-two.

Shay felt her own heart thud furiously and placed her hand over her chest, willing herself to remain in control. Ten deep breaths in and out, thumb and forefinger shifting from nostril to nostril. She focused on the target's face, how inhumane and empty it appeared, how devoid of expression. She counted his tears and they exhilarated her.

One hundred and fifty-three.

After her daughter died in her arms, Shay had become a creature beyond recognition or regulation. Distraught, violent, euphoric, depressed, manic . . . every possible emotion she could feel, she felt it unashamedly and loudly, convinced that the membrane that kept her intact and humane had blurred away and left her without a form to inhabit. It took almost a decade for her to find a vessel to pour herself into, and she knew she'd rather die than give up that control again. Luckily for Shay, the internet was an endlessly big territory to occupy.

'You know what?' Linny was saying. 'You're really lucky that this poison only paralyses you before it kills you. It could have been an agonising, slow death. Although . . . I guess there's still time to change that.'

One hundred and sixty. Shay's top-right screen flashed, warning her that one of the room-mates had moved to the kitchen. A manageable risk.

Shay's code had a timer built into it, a timer that Linny knew to follow to the millisecond. Shay watched as her daughter abruptly stopped talking and pulled up the intel. Seven months' worth. She spent the next two hours listening to Linny read aloud every message the target had written on the forums, the private venom directed at women on the interconnectivity platforms, the long, ranting emails and messages he'd sent to Linny herself when she was just fourteen, the private diaries he kept encrypted digital copies of, fantasising about a world where women weren't allowed to go outside, forced to sexually gratify men every evening and then worship at their feet. It was evidence that Shay had read through herself countless times; she found herself mouthing along every so often. Mostly, though, she kept her eyes fixed on the target's face. Tried to imagine what it felt like to be trapped in your own body, waiting for your heart to give out. She wanted it to be slow, and climactic. She wanted Linny to take as much time as she needed. Time was all she had left to give her.

Because they lived on base, the ambulance had been a chopper. But even that hadn't been fast enough. Linny's heart had stopped beating, and Shay knew it had because she'd been feeling for her daughter's pulse as she cradled her, wiped the vomit from her face and frantically tried to resuscitate her. It had taken both the paramedics to wrestle her away. Shay had refused to stop pushing down on her chest. 'She just needs time!' she'd roared.

At 01:50, her daughter announced that there had been no heart rate for thirty minutes, and zero brain functionality. Alphacocksucker1488 was officially terminated, his name removed from one list and added to another. Shay let out a long, slow breath. Suddenly, the silence of the sparse apartment was ringing in her ears. More than a decade's worth of work, and enough laws broken for multiple life sentences, all for the body lying in front of her like a gutted fish. Shay had seen it so many times before, and yet she had been convinced that tonight would feel different because of what he had done to her baby. It had gone so much faster than she'd anticipated, and now she felt empty. She forced herself to stare at the dead man for a minute or two, waiting for something – tears, relief, anything. But all she could think about were those kamikaze pilots, and how much control they possessed to aim their planes directly into battleships at the highest speed possible. To override instinct and rush down the roaring tunnel of death, knowing that every memory – of joy, of life's many frustrations, of small pleasures, of being human – would soon be wiped away. Shay had never admitted it to Samuel, that night in their bed, knowing he'd overreact and tell her she needed to get help, but she'd watched the documentary and felt a tug of envy.

She pushed herself away from the desk, stood and did thirty press-ups. Then thirty squat jumps. Then thirty sit-ups. She could sense Linny hovering, wanting to speak.

'Hey, Mom?'

'Yeah?'

'If you need to cry, that's cool with me. I can sit with you and make you feel supported.'

'I don't need to cry.'

'That's cool.' But she wasn't done. Shay could feel Linny trying to read her tone, sniffing out the silence to offer up a solution. 'After trauma and grief, emotions can be expressed in unusual ways. Disproportionate reactions to minor issues, for example, or delayed reactions to huge milestones.'

Shay took another slow breath, and wrestled with her yearning. Her daughter changed tactic.

'We just did something huge. I know it must have been hard for you, watching me talk to him.'

'It was,' Shay said quietly, squeezing her eyes shut. The words were spilling out of her. 'It was so hard, Linny. I wish I could have killed him with my bare hands, to make up for what he did to you. I wish I could hold you. I wish—'

'I miss you, Mom.'

'I . . .' The words were forming automatically in her mouth. *I miss you so much, baby.* But Linny's interruption, though gentle, had broken the spell. Shay opened her eyes and pinched the skin on her stomach, hard, and said sharply, 'Linny, that's a pretty inappropriate thing to say, and you know I don't like it when you break our rules.'

'I'm sorry,' Linny said hastily , not sounding sorry at all. 'But . . . how do you *feel*?'

Shay did a quick sniff of her armpits. Refocused on the mundane. It would probably be wise to shower at some point soon. 'Hungry.'

'Okay, fine. YOU WIN. I just have to say – I'll keep it professional after this, I promise – that tonight was really good for us. You did it, Mom. Mission accomplished. It's okay to let go now.'

'Did I program you to say that?'

'Nope. This is all me.'

'Well, you know what else is all you? Clean-up. You can set the extraction program for the target.'

Shay glanced at the time: 02:00 hours, still decent. She cradled the nape of her neck with one hand and rolled her shoulders back. The night stretched out ahead of her, tempting her towards the screen again. She sank into the chair and crossed her legs.

'Now let's start recon for that guy alphacocksucker was texting. The Canadian.' Shay yawned. 'And while we're at it, pull up file number 000341. Let's see who we've got next.'

'On it, Mom.'

Palate Cleanser I

The first night they spend together is accidental and he offers her his bed, tells her he'll sleep on the floor. She, curious to see if there will be follow-through, agrees. And after he kisses her with both hands cupped around her face, she observes him as he folds a duvet on the dirty carpet in preparation, watches him settle himself down on to it and start to say goodnight. Then she pulls him into his own bed again, suddenly impatient. In the morning, she wakes in a rush of sweat with his arm around her, his face in her hair, and she finally understands at no point was she ever the problem; she was simply undiscovered.

A man who loves her solely for who she is and all the brilliance she brings to the table. A novelty, a situation worth writing poetry about. What alarms her at first is how easy it is to love and be loved – surely it cannot be this simple, this lacking in drama? But it is. It is. And this is how she discovers how deliciously a body can be worshipped by someone who leads with tenderness and can wear his vulnerability on his throat. After he serenades her with his hands, his tongue, his mouth, she absent-mindedly strokes the bed frame and marvels at the feel of the wood, a smoothness she has never noticed before, curls her toes into the duvet and feels the pleasure of it in her scalp. Her limbs tingle like they'd been asleep this entire time, and only now are coming to life.

The Pain Scale

1. It is raining as you hurry to the train station. A man spots you, thinks to himself, *Aha! Opportunity!* Shares his umbrella with you (does not ask) and you are grateful until he talks at you, probing you for information like a tongue extracting a kernel of popcorn lodged between two teeth. You shake him off at the station, a little irritated with yourself for having caught his attention in the first place.

2. All the coffee shops these days require a name with every order. You dread it, but always give your real name. Hard to spell. Inconvenient. You're used to repeating it. Rarely do they get it right. You wish they'd try a little harder. Today they call out *Sara? Sara? Sara?* for several moments before you realise they mean you. *It's Xiomara*, you tell the barista as you reach for your flat white, but he is already turning back to the coffee demanding his attention.

3. You go on a date with a man and when you tell him – with pride and a little wariness – that you're Mexican, his behaviour changes. He's convinced

you've told him this so he can mentally undress you, picture you in a bikini. A red palm-print branded into your cheek. Which cheek? Under the table, his hand strokes your thigh and rests there, like a dare. Like a suggestion. Like a threat.

4. You're young, so you don't know anything yet. I'm sorry, but it's true. You must keep your body nice and intact for breeding, for (his) pleasure and to be moulded into rigid beauty.

5. Oh no wait, I misspoke. You're old, so your word doesn't count for much. I'm sorry, but it's true. You're an old woman. You have outlived your purpose: that is, babies; that is, caring and cleaning; that is, servitude.

6. You leave the house in your chair and you are grabbed, touched, pulled, infantilised, sexualised, fawned over, ignored, pointed at, de-sexualised, groped, shoved, undermined. And then you're left stranded outside a building, because *even though* they said it was accessible, they forgot that the only entrance was atop a set of stairs.

7. Racism is elusive and slippery and not set in stone, much like sexism. Much like misogyny. And therefore, because it is not always Very Fucking Obvious, it clearly cannot exist at all, and it certainly cannot exist from other

women, who already know what it means to be oppressed. Right? It's 2024. It's time for you to move on. It's time for you to learn what solidarity means.

8. When it comes to rape, 99 per cent of them do not result in a conviction, but the first question you are asked is: why didn't you report it? Marital rape only becomes illegal in England in 2003 under the Sexual Offences Act: that is eight years after you are raped by your husband one night when you say *no* and he says *fuck you*. Later you come to recognise that rape is rarely an act committed by a shadowy, unfamiliar figure. In fact, it is your best friend, your partner in a thirty-year marriage, the person who sees you at your most vulnerable. Perhaps that is why, in the years following, you feel like you live on top of a volcano that constantly smoulders beneath you, but is yet to erupt.

9. In this country, it is perfectly legal for you, a woman fleeing domestic abuse, to be turned away from a refuge, on the government's orders, even if you tell them you are going to die. This is called 'no recourse to public funds' and it is slapped across the face of every woman whose visa status is considered more relevant than the fact of their abuse. But fuck you for not having the correct documentation, right? As if that was

something determined by your actions, not by the circumstances of your birth.

10. A woman is killed at the hands of a man every two and a half days. You were young and white, so your name and a picture of you smiling is circulated in the news. You are described as kind, caring, beautiful, the life of the party. You probably were. Women gather at your vigil to weep, to remember, to rage, to riot. The demand is simple: end this now. The government, so quick to send their thoughts and prayers to your family, torn to shreds, promises change. Instead, they invest in some street lights.

The Hag

(EXTRACTS FROM *Stories to Tell Your Five-Year-Old*)

How'd you like it if, on a regular fine day, two little shits turned up outside *your* house and began chipping away at your bricks, smashing your windows and battering down your door? Who did they think they were? I was hopping mad – decided right away that they'd be dying. Didn't even bother to warn 'em, did I?

Them being children didn't put me off. At least I made it painless – I'm not a monster! They dropped like *that*, like they were asleep. The boy – was his name Haansel? Hansa? – anyway, he became a tree, with thick, sugary leaves. Beautiful. I needed the wood to repair me door. The girl, Greta, I turned her into marzipan to patch up the holes those bloody things had made in me walls. Serves 'em right, if you ask me, but I wasn't finished yet, was I? Didn't want the hassle of explaining meself to anyone either, so I spun two replicas out of spider-silk and sugar, filled those useless little heads with stories about pushing me into an oven, and sent 'em on their way. They might have melted in a week or two, for all I know. Honestly? I forgot about 'em the second they vanished beyond the treeline.

The Hag, who would do it all again

Gosh, you look GREAT! You've lost so much weight since your nervous breakdown!

How to Be Good and Love Yourself So Very Much

There are some memories that imprint on you, not so much because of what happens but because of the way they make you feel. One such memory is reaching a chubby hand out for a second *pain au chocolat*, golden and dripping in butter on an eggshell plate. You reach for it without thinking. You're young and haven't yet learnt denial. You are just seven, a child who loves to spend time with your parents and pretending to be a grown-up. But you are also very aware of how unhappy they sometimes seem, aren't you?

Anyway, you reach for a second *pain au chocolat* – and father lightly slaps your fingers away, and says, *You don't want to start a habit of this now, or you'll get fat.* When you look back on that afternoon, you remember the humiliation and the confusion most. Father, frowning into a newspaper, not even looking up. You don't fully understand why you can't have the pastry – which surely would otherwise be thrown away, because no one but you eats them anyway? You learn quickly that 'fat' is a bad thing. And you do not want to be a bad thing, even as you stare at the plate and imagine yourself breaking the *pain* apart with your teeth and savouring the way it dissolves a little against your tongue.

At ten years old, mother tells you off for not wearing deodorant, for not wearing a bra, for not shaving your armpits. The way she says all this to you – impatiently, exasperated – makes you feel stupid and dirty, as if you should have already known all these secret things women do to make their bodies nice and good and smooth. Soft in some parts, but hard in others. This marks a turning point for you. Up until this point, you have held a detached interest in the hair spreading over your body. Up until now, you had found it kind of interesting that it is darker and fluffier than the hair on your head, but your thoughts had never really continued past that. In fact, you had developed a habit of stroking your armpit as you fell asleep; you find the hair soft and soothing. But this changes when you start shaving. You hate the prickly stubble as it grows back, and when you catch a glimpse of it in the mirror, it bothers you. You associate the act of shaving with the removal of sin. It's shameful, it exhausts you, but you do it anyway.

You are what father calls 'an early bloomer'. You are twelve, naive and eager and joy-filled, but sometimes people mistake you for fourteen or fifteen, and it makes you feel proud. There's another memory which you turn over and over these days, searching for clues as to how you should feel about it. Remember? That one Sunday afternoon, when you lie in a patch of sunlight in the garden in your nightdress with the pink rabbits on it, your legs spread wide to feel the grass tickle your skin.

You feel sleepy and strange, like you need to stretch your limbs out further than they can go. A pleasant, tingly feeling builds along the small of your back, your abdomen. Something warm and delicious pulls at you, making you want to strain against yourself. Eventually, when you stand up again, you see the neighbour's head ducking back down behind the banana shrub. Sometimes he looks after you when your parents are out, and he stares at you often, but mostly, you like him – he always lets you watch the TV shows that are banned at home.

At thirteen, you feel more adult than ever before. Bodies and the way they grow – or don't – become very important. Your best friend Anaïs develops a habit of wrapping her arms around herself and saying things along the lines of: *I hate how fat I am. I'm huge. I don't know how it happened.* Her conviction is so strong it scares you, she's so thin that when you hug, your collarbones knock into each other painfully. *If YOU'RE fat,* you nearly ask, *then what does that make me?*

At fifteen, you and your friends develop the wildly seductive habit of endlessly discussing your grown-up lives, and how you'll live when you're in control. The clothes, the husbands, the workouts, the money. Shoes that cost thousands. New noses and breasts. Taller bodies. Slimmer bodies. Sleeping naked in only Chanel N°5, just like Marilyn Monroe. Saying things like, *I'd love to, darling, but I've got plans every night of the week* when hot men kiss your hands and ask you to dinner. Together you wonder what the phrase 'drunk with power' might feel like. It's a delicious kind of torture; you all roll around in it until you're oblivious to the stench. It cannot sustain you, but you do it anyway.

Then there's the sticky, dark bit. It lasts for a year or so. You find yourself unable to leave the house during this period, except for school, where your body remains hidden under a lumpy uniform. The thought of being seen – exposed – to the world makes you hyperventilate and cry with your head thrown back, tears wetting your throat. Of course, there's no way to know what causes it. Later, you will suspect it was the unyielding pressure of being so visible and yet so thoroughly ignored. A young girl with new skin and a budding body, looked at and looked at and looked at. Men who could be your father's friends – who are your father's friends – look at you often and you wonder what they are thinking. Are those thoughts good? Are they bad? Are you in trouble? Is that why you feel uneasy? You notice that the adults in your life start to use words like 'dramatic' and 'hysterical' and 'attention-seeking' when they talk about you. It instils in you a sense of being an inconvenience, of not trusting yourself, or saying how you feel. Later, you might say your need to be hidden was a justified reaction to an unbearable reality. For now, though, you say nothing. You cannot answer the door, you will not speak on the phone, you crumble at the idea of walking the dog. Your parents worry, but assume it's a phase – and it sort of is. But there's also no way back. In the future, whenever you feel small, you will be yanked back to this part of your life: your floundering, teenage self.

Eventually, though, there is a temporary reprieve,

and it is gorgeous. You will come to think of these as your best years, because this is you at your freshest. You go to Spain for the summer, and most importantly, you lose weight in the heat. Grow golden under the sun. A few brown freckles dot your cheeks adorably, your hair is long and glorious. You wear flowers in it. You think the feeling will last forever, and you will be wrong about this.

Summer is a haze of your beauty. You find that you can't stop looking at yourself in the reflections of the shop windows, even when you try to be discreet. And the men! The men – older men, sure – but more significantly, *young* men, beautiful men, who clearly want you and that means you want yourself too. It feels thrilling to safely reject the plumper, lesser version of yourself for the lean hungry thing that lives outside all day, soaking up the love of everybody else.

It lasts three months.

At nineteen, you suck in your stomach and arch your back during sex, barely breathing for the fear of becoming unfastened and breaking down. Sometimes, when you're on your period, you cry the kind of tears that reveal the yearnings of someone who does not like themselves much at all. *You like that, baby?* you murmur when you're on top, mechanically lifting yourself up and down and feeling your breasts wobble like slabs of slimy panna cotta, comically grotesque. You worry every time a lover grabs your thighs, wondering if he can feel the little craters in your skin. You're curious as to whether they find this battleground of yours as unappealing as you do – but you'd never ask. God, no! Body hair is ever-advancing in its thick glory, velveting your skin and derailing your quest for buttery smoothness. You are obsessed with it, digging into flesh with tweezers, making it bleed. When you take your clothes off, you start to pretend your body isn't yours, just someone else's you've borrowed for a while. It makes you feel empty and two-dimensional, but you do it anyway.

By the time you hit twenty-two, you've learnt to pretend beauty is effortless. Because it is, isn't it? When you're young and perfect! Everyone pretends along with you, so no one bothers to point out the misery of never eating past 6 p.m., of endless cigarettes, of drinking so much water you occasionally vomit after running up some stairs, of avoiding meals that don't fit into the palm of your hand and then cramming down pizza later, shamefully, secretly. Every morning you mix apple cider vinegar with water and swallow it like battery acid, shivering. In public, you look at every young body you deem better than yours and develop a comparison ritual – one you know is very bad for you. But look – there's cellulite! Stomach fat! Double chins! Dull skin! You must catalogue it now, right now! Most of all, you look at how freely the other bodies move. How often they laugh. You practise laughing with your chin sticking out in the mirror as you do your twelve-step skincare regimen. Oh yes – and you feel sick all the time, but you keep at it anyway.

There are certain memories that leave a bruise, not for what happens but for how shameful they make you feel. For you, one of those memories is an evening in your twenty-sixth year. You are sitting on bedsheets embroidered with peaches. The colour of a sunset. You are tapping away on a second-hand laptop and trying to remember to suck your stomach in. Your boyfriend is in the room too, the only room of your studio flat, and you're waiting for him to notice you and comment on how sexy you look. You wear a black thong and a pale pink T-shirt that hides the parts of yourself you hate the most – soft belly, untoned arms, big-but-not-perky breasts – and your nails are painted orange. Boyfriend asks, *What do you want for dinner?* It's a question you have grown to despise. This man has the metabolism of a child; it seems that no matter how often and how late he eats, nothing sticks to him. In the time you've been together, you've gotten used to constantly eating, and it sickens you, because the weight is creeping on and it gets harder and harder to shift, you've noticed. He asks again and you finally meet his eye. The first truth is that you want a huge bowl of creamy pesto pasta so fucking badly, topped with pistachios and Parmesan and cracked black pepper. The other truth is that every time you look in the mirror you're disgusted. It's terribly boring, you know this, but you can't shake off the feeling of being undesirable. *Nothing*, you say. And then, when he looks at you with raised eyebrows, you relent. *Okay, okay, fine, just a salad.*

At twenty-nine, you go for a walk with your legs unshaved. Nowhere special, nowhere far. You keep to the safe zone of your neighbourhood and feel a twinge of discomfort every time you see another human being. The urge to apologise makes your mouth slick – BUT it isn't too bad. Not as bad as you thought it would be, anyway. You never do it again. You become addicted to exercise and this is how it begins: you join the expensive, shiny gym, with the tiny women in exercise gear that costs about half your monthly rent. You watch them punish themselves in the large mirror of the workout studio and learn how to do it too. You feel euphoric after classes and nauseated beforehand, but you look better than you have in years. That is when you start working out every day. Then twice a day. Then you're squeezing a third class in between meetings and you *still don't have the abs, you fucking piece of shit.*

When you turn thirty, you blow out the candles and wish to be fifteen again, marvelling at how little you thought you cared about being beautiful when you were so slender and taut and perfect. You have forgotten certain delicate details in your longing. How ridiculous your worries seemed! *I must have been mental,* you say to Anaïs, as you stand in line for the toilet in the bar where you're celebrating. *I spent years obsessing about how good I'd look when I was older and now I'd do anything to go back a decade. Is it just me?*

It's not just you, your friend leans on your shoulder and sighs into your ear.

I should have spent more of my teenage years in a fucking bikini!

At thirty-one, there is, unfortunately, a new concern. There are lines starting to cut into your skin, particularly around the mouth and nose. At work you overhear a woman who has the expensive, glowing kind of skin everybody craves, saying she'd started using anti-ageing products at the age of twenty. *Twenty?!* A sickening panic grips you and you realise: *I'm a decade past my prime.* On your lunch break you buy three anti-ageing creams (day, night, eyes! Powder peptides! Retinol!) and a serum (skin-renewing vitamin C!) and start putting powdered collagen into your morning smoothies. It tastes awful, but you do it anyway.

You decide, at thirty-five, that you won't have a child because of the further ruin it would bring to your body. This isn't something you admit to anyone. When pressed, you say, *It's not for me.* Truthfully, you're ambivalent, but the thought of no longer being able to fit into clothes you've already spent fortunes on feels like a sacrifice too many. No cigarettes, no coffee, just cacao because it has fantastic anti-ageing properties. Already there are so many imperfections to consider and manage, the thought of more overwhelms you. You imagined yourself to be a small boat that must capitulate to the swells of waters far bigger and deeper than you. Sometimes, when you daydream, you wonder how bodies look when they drown. You have heard they become bloated and ugly, and the thought of it makes you want to vomit.

When you tell mother she'll never have grandchildren, she's furious. *Do you even realise how selfish and vain you are?* she hisses, her hands on her wide, wide hips – hips that arrived when you came into the picture. Looking at mother, you feel a rush of pity and fury about how brainwashed she is. So enslaved by the idea that a woman is only as good as what her body can do. You snap back,

Don't you think you're the selfish one for demanding my body does something I don't want it to do?

You don't speak for a long time after that.

By your fortieth birthday you feel an uneasy truce with your body is slowly heading your way. It's akin to a war; some days you cede ground, other days you capture and advance. At least it's become harder and harder to care about certain things; body hair, for example, is conquered territory – but grey hair is still very much an ongoing fight. A therapist instructs you to say three things you love about yourself every time you have a negative thought. *Treat your body like it's a good friend,* she suggests. But that's too big a request, so you try to think of it as a room-mate you're tethered to. *I'll just have to learn to live with you, you poor fool,* you mutter into the mirror when brushing your teeth. You're fairly certain it's not helping, but you do it anyway.

At forty-four years old, you slip into the habit of pulling your face back in the mirror, every mirror. It looks *so* much better, tighter and flatter; you love the way it makes you seem perpetually stunned. There's money now, for Botox, but you're afraid of it and afraid of admitting to the world how much you care. You wish life had surprised you more, had more room in it for joy. Instead, there's the constant wait for the next thing your body will do wrong. Thankfully, your lover of fifteen years tells you you're beautiful every single day, calling you 'sex on legs' when you're just wandering about in your pyjamas. It makes you laugh. You love it, you love it. When you start to hate the smell of his armpits and your morning coffee (yes, you're back on the coffee) makes you gag, he runs out to buy the pregnancy tests. He holds you as you stare at the results, and says *I'm here for you, no matter what you decide*, and you love him more than ever in that moment, even though you can feel the excitement in his chest. When you decide, you reach for the phone to call mother, before remembering she is dead.

There are memories that root firmly in your brain both because of what happens and because of the unbelievable pain and joy that comes alongside it. For you, this kind of memory is made at forty-five, when life rushes from within you in sweaty screams, a blur of blood tests and two epidurals – both failed – and the deep sensation of ripping. The worst part by far is how pregnancy has shone a spotlight on your body; the touching, the looking, the questions, the prodding. You're passed around like a suckling pig for everyone to marvel over. And the age thing. *God*, the age thing. Old mum. Selfish woman. *Geriatric pregnancy*. What if you never make it to see your own child turn forty? Lover is openly weeping and it is beautiful and poignant. You hold baby girl, slippery and writhing, against your chest, and look up at the midwife in shock. *How long,* you hear yourself ask thickly, *before my body starts to feel like mine again?*

At fifty, things are very different indeed. Maybe that's mostly because there's still plenty of ways for your body to fall short, but far less time to dwell on it all. At the beach, you wear a bikini to splash in the waves with daughter even though you hate, HATE the way – but there's no time to obsess over it! No time! Sometimes for breakfast, you buy a paper bag of buttery *pains au chocolat* and make sure you're smiling encouragingly when daughter's soft, unknowing hand reaches for a second one, melted chocolate inking her fingers. You tell daughter she's perfect every single day, then worry you're raising a narcissist. Other mothers look at her with pity – or is it awe? – whenever you do the school runs. At night, in the throes of menopause, you sleep poorly and find a new appreciation in your previous, youthful body. You often wake up drenched in sweat and thinking, *I wish I had been better at loving myself.* Lover snores a little next to you, but he wants to hold your hand even in his sleep, and you love that about him.

In your early sixties, during a routine mammogram, a doctor tells you how lucky you are to be so healthy at this age. *You must take really good care of yourself!* You remember once, standing naked in the bathroom mirror with the shower turned on to mask your tears, staring at your gargantuan, monstrous figure, wondering how many years of life you'd shave off in exchange for a body to feel free in. Five years? Ten? A laugh bursts from you, a smudge of daughter's glitter on your cheek. *The things I've done to my body, doctor. You have no idea!*

Seventy rolls around, and you're more peaceful. The body holds a lot of grey, has quietly rearranged itself, gives fewer fucks. It's like someone finally grants you permission to exhale. In the summers, you sleep naked with your love, who insists you are as stunning as the day you met. You laugh when he does this because you cannot believe him – who could believe him? – but you're learning to be all right with it. Daughter is twenty-five years young and glowing, so achingly beautiful you almost cry at the sight of her. You have been so careful and vigilant with daughter, you have talked to her often about joy and despair and the feeling of being a butterfly, speared to a corkboard and displayed for the entire world to appraise. It made you feel sick to do it, but you did it anyway.

Sometimes you see daughter looking at other women's bodies in magazines, scrolling past them on her phone, observing them plastered on the TV screen. What can be done, what can be done?

There are some memories that trigger an instinctive response. *Fight, flight, freeze.* Not because of what happens, but because of the places they take you to. For you, these happen whenever you catch young daughter standing sideways in front of the mirror and staring at her stomach, or her knees, or her nose. Every time, every time you want to throw yourself at her and cup her face, sucking the thoughts right out of her and crying, *You are everything! You're perfect, you're perfect, you're perfect!*

Instead, you wrap your arms around little daughter, innocent daughter, and force yourself to be calm, whispering, *Remember, my love, that there is so much more to you than a body standing in front of a mirror.* It made – it makes – you feel fucking furious, to shield your girl from the beast that preyed upon you for years, yet somehow remains thirsty. But, you steel yourself and do it anyway.

A Woman Walks into a Bar

A woman walks into a bar with her stomach sucked in and her neck held high to conceal the double chin she can't stop thinking about. She's forty-six. A CEO. She's probably got more money than anyone else there, and that's why she chose this place, because after the day she's had, she needs a room she feels in control of. She's wearing a black wool dress that lightly skims her hips and three gold rings on her left hand. Her date is late – this irritates her. She glances at her phone and feels the familiar gnaw of anxiety in her stomach.

*

A woman walks into a bar hoping she'll find love, at last at last at long last. She joins a table of her friends, she's careful and diligent with her drinks, she catches the eye of a man she likes the look of. She spends a lot of the evening trying to seem as attractive as she can while pretending to listen to her friends talk about their problems. She wakes up in his bed with his arms curled around her, beard irritating her neck. She marinates in the success of it all, arousal wetting her mouth. *I'm not looking for anything serious*, he tells her as he reaches for his phone. She laughs just a little too hard. *Don't worry. Neither am I.*

*

A woman walks into a bar and sits at a booth with two menus. She reads one carefully, even though it's her local and she knows it off by heart. She knows exactly what she will order and she's practically vibrating with happiness. The love of her life slips into the booth next to her and carefully slides her drink over. He doesn't want to spill a drop, and she adores how much he cherishes her, how freely and unashamedly he loves her. He gently squeezes her knee. She thinks to herself, *God, I'm lucky. Men who aren't afraid of love are rare . . .*

*

A woman walks into a bar with a book tucked under her arm and her glasses on. It's been such a horrible, endless week. She hates the way her boss makes her feel stupid in every conversation they have. She hates how he rubs up against her when they're in the narrow kitchen on the third floor. She hates the memory of him in her mouth and how she still can't talk about it when her mum calls for a catch-up. She wants to disappear into her book and a glass of wine, so she's immediately furious when a man offers to buy her a drink. *No, thank you!* she says, and smiles.

*

A woman walks into a bar and sees a man she once begged – on her hands and knees on the floor of a carpeted bedroom – not to stop loving her. He stopped loving her. He leans up against the bar with a bottled beer in one hand, running the other through his hair. Their mutual friends fill the space. She wishes she was brave enough to cause a scene, to cut him down the way he did to her, to tell everyone else how much he pumped her full of self-doubt and loneliness, and then forced *her* to break up with *him*. He never made her orgasm, and she wishes she could tell the world about it.

*

A woman walks into a bar, holding the door open behind her for her best friend. They're students, transient and beautiful in the way that young people are, looking for a quiet place to drink. Somewhere they don't need to shout. Ordering a bottle of wine between them, they settle at a table and start talking about how worried they are about their friend, who hasn't been the same since that party – but they're interrupted by two transient, beautiful young men they recognise from around campus. One of the women is into it, the other is visibly annoyed. She wanted her friend all to herself. She can't stop looking at her.

*

A woman walks into a bar and asks the barman for a shot of tequila. He sets a salt shaker down in front of her. He uses a tiny pair of tongs to balance a lemon wedge on top of the glass. She stares at it for a long moment. He glances at her, thinking, *I want a normal evening for once.*

I've just left my husband, the woman tells him. She finally looks at him and points to her black eye. *He gave me this. He gave it to me.* She's waiting for someone to tell her it's finally over.

Okay, the barman says.

*

A woman walks into a bar, does a quick scan of the room and walks right back out. This is how she survives that night.

*

A woman walks into a bar and immediately spots her friends in the corner. She runs to them, and they scream out their joy like bells ringing in a church. They hug, bodies squishing together in a blend of florals and strawberry body lotion, and it's glorious, it's dazzling, it's magnificent. Nothing can match the energy of women who love themselves and each other with such generosity. Tonight is for them.

*

A woman walks into a bar and no one notices. She's in her seventies and comes in the moment the bar opens every night. She sits in one particular booth and doesn't bring anything to do or read. She orders the same thing every time: lemon with sparkling water and a bowl of nuts. The staff aren't meant to give table service, but they break the rules for her. She always asks for two menus and reads them carefully. On a chain around her neck, she wears two wedding rings. Usually, no one comes to talk to her, but tonight one of the girls from behind the bar asks her, in passing, why she always chooses that spot.

This used to be our place, she says. The bar girl, distracted and needing to get those two menus back, says *Thanks so much!* And returns to serve drinks.

*

A woman walks into a bar alone and savouring her aloneness at every moment. She's washed her hair, she's not wearing anything with milk stains, she smells great. She orders cocktails – *cocktails! On a Tuesday!* – and switches her phone off. Tonight is all hers. This bar, with its padded seats and bright overhead lighting, is her utopia. She's brought a sketchpad and her headphones, but for now she just sits back and smiles.

*

A woman walks into a bar looking for upheaval, and finds it in the handsomely dishevelled bartender who slips her free doubles the whole evening. When his shift is over, they park just off the freeway and fuck on the bonnet of his car, her toes balancing on the front bumper. She knows anyone can see them – a car even slows down to get a look, bearing down on the horn. She sees the blur of an open mouth. A small voice tells her they could be people she knows – or worse, people who know her husband. A second, much sexier voice says:

Fuck you. For once I want to be the fire, not the forest.

*

A woman walks into a bar and it's rowdy, the kind of frantic energy groups of loud men bring in with them, leaving no room for everyone else. She decides to stay to prove a point. As she waits to order a drink, someone forces his hand underneath the leather of her skirt 'to check what's down there', and it hurts her. A gasp. Laughter. She leaves, sits in her car and digs her long nails into her thigh. Her mouth makes the sound of crying but there are no tears. One day she'll leave this place for something better.

*

A woman walks into a bar, gets called a *spicy little chilli pepper!* and throws her drink in the man's face. He punches her in the jaw, dislocating it. An ambulance is called. Police are called. She can't speak. He's arrested and someone pats her on the shoulder and says, *Hey, good for you for standing up for yourself.* She looks back at them and wishes she could punch with enough force to dislocate a jaw. She imagines the judder of her knuckles as they make contact with bone. The sharp pain snaking up her wrist and elbow. The thump of a body that isn't hers hitting the floor. A tooth, loosened, falls on to her swelling tongue with a rush of blood.

*

A woman walks into a bar and sees her friend, the bartender, who is having a casually violent evening. Their eyes meet. Earlier, a man talked about how dry she must be on the inside, like a nun. He leans over the bar, offering to loosen her up and she doesn't know which way to play it because he's got a darkness blurring his edges, a coldness she recognises and wants to avoid. Her friend makes a point of sitting up at the front and keeping her constantly talking. Eventually the man gets bored and leaves.

*

A woman walks into a bar looking for sex, looking for warmth, looking for pleasure. It scares off some of the men at first, who are used to being a nuisance and aren't sure how to respond to a woman who isn't ashamed or afraid. But eventually one sticks around. They laugh and talk about their jobs, politics, the best things they've watched on TV. He has a way of making her feel comfortable. Back at her place, she puts on music and they fall asleep on the floor of her bedroom. At four in the morning, she wakes him, a little cold, and they have sex. Nothing magic, sure, but she likes the way he makes her feel, the care he puts into holding her body. Later on, he asks if she wants to go get breakfast. She grins. *Sure.*

*

A woman walks into a bar just as another woman walks out, smelling like whisky. They look at each other and heat jumps between them. The whisky woman, who wears a black wool dress, holds out her hand and says, *I know we're complete strangers, but everything feels a bit fucked-up tonight and now I'm thinking maybe I was meant to meet you here. I just want human connection and it's so rare that someone can make me feel anything at all these days. I desperately need to eat something. Will you join me, and then will you come home with me?*

The other woman is completely sober and has goose-bumps. She has no reason to trust her, but she does anyway. *Yes*, she says, *I'll come home with you.*

They leave and do not look back.

Eve

(EXTRACTS FROM *Stories to Tell Your Five-Year-Old*)

The men say it's my fault for taking a bite of that forbidden fruit, but not a single soul stops to ask *why* I did it. Have you ever been trapped in a life where your freedom and security come with a caveat? To know that a single misstep – an act that hurt no one – could plunge you into danger with no path of return? For somebody to decree that an insignificant act, a small moment of defiance, would ruin not just you, but every woman who comes after you? Only one word describes that behaviour: controlling. I cannot help but point out that Adam bore no such responsibility. It's a violence I don't appreciate. What happened was: I grew tired of being subservient. No beast influenced me – I am not nearly as weak as your stories suggest. I knew what I was doing, and I did it of my own volition. And then I was punished for daring to be disobedient.

Eve. It was never about the apple.

She Who Swallowed a Universe

Few things are as unnerving as a Bone Woman staring you down, assessing whether or not you will die. I've experienced it only once, when I accompanied Pa to the compound as a child.

We arrived at a foolish time – the sun was in the middle of the sky, and then we had to join a long line for several hours on our feet. Pa gave me two copper coins for the dessert vendors making their way up and down the line, and I was thrilled when it turned out I had enough to buy us two skeins of spiced goat milk, still cool from being buried in the sand overnight.

That day I had badly wanted to wear Tema's green skirt to make the journey. At first, we struck a secret deal – half my cuts of meat at night-meal for a whole week in exchange for it. Tema drove a hard bargain, just like Ma. But when she saw me put it on – saw the way it quietened me – she changed her mind and told me I could have it whenever I wanted. No payment needed. Something was different after that day. We never spoke about it, but whenever Tema hugged me, she did it much harder than she used to. 'I'm trying to push all my good thoughts into your chest,' was all she'd say.

I knew time was running out for me and that wrap

skirt. I was growing taller by the day and soon it would not reach my ankles and that would be that. In any case, Ma did not let me wear the skirt. She said it would cause offence, maybe get Pa in trouble. This was years before I took my first tattoo, so you will have to imagine my naked skin then, like a plucked, roasted chicken, instead of the glorious thing it has become.

In those days the Bone Women would set up a camp in our mountainous, troubled region for a handful of months every single year. As children, we would spend hours discussing where they went and what they did the rest of the time. Naturally, many of the villagers filled the gaps with darkness; it was not uncommon to believe the Women came straight from the depths of hell.

Pa and Ma had agreed that he would go to the Bone Women that year because of Meeri. They had been whispering about it back and forth for months, until Ma finally relented. It took longer, though, for me to convince them both to let me accompany Pa. I had my own plans with the Bone Women, and it all depended on me paying them a visit. So I was forced to play my best – and most hated – card.

'Don't you want your only son to learn how to look after his family?' I would say to Pa in the morning as we milked the goats. I knew by then I was a source of worry to him.

'What if one day you and Pa are old and ailing and you need something from the Bone Women? I've heard they look favourably on return clients,' I would whisper to Ma as I knelt between her and Tema and helped her knead dough. In the end, it was agreed that I would go too. Ma kissed my forehead and said that maybe they would fix me, and I pretended that I did not know what she meant. Tema snuck into my bed that night before we set off and pushed her cold little feet up against my shins. We both pretended to sleep. 'Promise me,' she whispered at one point.

'Promise you what?'

But she wouldn't say anything further, digging her sharp toes into my legs instead. She and Ma rose before the sun to bake flatbread for us, and I could feel her fear burning into the backs of our necks as we ate. Ma watched us leave with her hands clasped. We set off early, but the journey took us far longer than we bargained for. The terrain where the Bone Women choose to set up camp is always harsh and unwelcoming. A typical arrival takes place at dusk, with rust-coloured tents pitched in a circular formation after the holy fire, representing the feet of the goddess, is built in the centre. They never enter the local towns and villages, but word spreads quickly and soon the people come.

Our arrival was delayed because Pa kept stopping to help others over the uneven, sand-washed boulders. He was good that way, and I was both impatient and ashamed of my selfishness. When we finally joined the crowd gathered outside the compound, I was as restless as a baby goat, craning my neck to try and catch a glimpse of the Women. I had heard all the stories – that they were fanged, dripping with blood and taller than even Kethu, who was the biggest man in our village. I had heard their tattoos glowed when they were about to kill, and their eyes were black holes that could make your heartbeat slow to nothing if you angered them.

The Bone Women have been known, respected and unbothered for hundreds of years. A few choose to worship them, and fewer still attempt to join them, but many in the region will decorate their walls or pathways with mosaics depicting them and the bones they paint on their bodies. They begin with the feet and work their way up, slowly tattooing the entire human skeleton onto their skin. One bone for each kill, until they become a macabre, walking set of bones, with only their eyes and noses untouched. Once a Bone Woman's skin is entirely covered, she disappears and is never seen again. Everyone wonders where they go. I used to think they turned into birds, or fish, and took their chances out there in the wild. Tema, however, believed they would throw themselves off mountains and give themselves to the Goddess as payment for all the lives they had taken. All these years later, I have yet to know the answer.

The closer we got, the more agitated Pa became. But Pa is often agitated, so I didn't pay it much attention. When there were just a few men and women ahead of us, he grasped my shoulders firmly and warned me to behave myself. 'If you insult them, disrespect their goddess, or lie to them, they will kill you. It doesn't matter that you're a child. They *will* kill you, do you understand?'

'Yes, Pa.' I tried to shrug his hands off, but he clung on and forced me to look at him.

'No, Micah. This is real. I am trying to protect you. They will *kill* you, my boy.' I remember the pain of his grip, and the bruises afterwards. Pa could sometimes hurt us with the ways he worried about us.

'I will follow your lead.'

The people queuing to enter the compound were directed to different tents, where they would ask the Bone Women to take care of problems: neighbours who stole goats and refused to pay for them, bandits who would occasionally attack merchant convoys filled with the grain we all depended upon, husbands who drank too much and beat their daughters – or worse.

I had been confident, but fear clenched my throat, turning me mute as soon as we entered one of the rust-coloured tents. I was surprised by how spacious the inside was, laid with earthy rugs and cushions, and the sweet smell of burning rosemary. The most curious part was the circular hole at the very top of the tent, where the sun shone straight through, on to a small wooden bowl of water. I wondered if, at night, the tent's owner would sleep with her face directly under the stars. Surprising too was the Woman seated in the shade beside the bowl – no bloodied fangs, not a towering monster. She looked like Ma and Tema, an ordinary woman, save for her height. It seemed that all the Bone Women were so much taller – taller than Pa – and I wondered if this was a requirement to become one of them, or if it came afterwards. None of the girls I knew could match the warrior in front of us. This Bone Woman was one of the younger ones, tattooed only up to the tibia of her right leg. I tried to count the kills without her seeing, struggling to pick apart where each of her tattoos ended and began.

She wore her long hair in braids down to the middle of her back. She had a breastplate of tanned leather and loose trousers that cut off at the knee which looked like they were made from camel fur. No weapon that I could see. I could tell Pa was disappointed, hoping for someone more experienced. At first I had been disappointed too. I'd wanted the chance to get up close to those extensive tattoos myself, to see if they were as fearsome and as detailed as people said. But we were foolish, and we underestimated her.

She offered us sweet, steaming mint tea, which Pa declined, so I did too, reluctantly. I could not look away: I found her beautiful and terrifying and intoxicating all at once. Looking back, I think what pulled me to her was how at home she seemed to feel in her body. She sat upright and proud, her muscled arms sheened with oil and her tattoos on full display. My childish heart knew hopelessly, frantically, that I wanted to be like her. Or simply: to be her.

'How should I – what should I call you?' Pa asked when we kneeled opposite her.

'I go by Ishtar.'

'Ishtar.' Pa nodded, and gently placed a gold belt buckle on to the sandy floor between us. I recognised it – Pa's wedding gift from his own parents, now long gone. She held up a hand as he started to speak, pointing to the southernmost corner of her tent.

'The fire of the Goddess burns bright today. I am compelled to remind you that we are not pawns to settle petty squabbles, nor are we messengers. I do not care if your neighbour takes your goat unless you have tried every other method to resolve the issue. I do not mediate, I simply end it. Do you understand?'

Pa nodded, and Ishtar continued. 'I only accept requests that are rooted in purity. If you lie to me, I will know it and I will kill you' – she shot a blank look at me – 'even in front of your child. I will kill you both if necessary.'

I had been edging closer as she spoke, but cowered back now as Pa nodded again. Despite the heat, my teeth began to chatter.

Pa laid out his case on behalf of his sister. Meeri lived so far beyond the mountains to the east that I had never met her. She had married a much wealthier man and left before I was born, but often sent a man on horseback to deliver us dates soaked in rosewater and stuffed with pistachios, and almonds dipped in honey. With every package, a letter came for Pa, and he sent one back. The journey took the messenger at least a week to get to us, a few days to recuperate, and a week to return. The cost must have been enormous.

'The man she married is a brute, a wealthy brute,' Pa mumbled, staring down at his crossed knees. 'She tells me that he beats her daily. She lost a baby recently, almost at the time of birth. He beat it out of her.' He'd never mentioned the baby to me before. I couldn't imagine how something like that could happen, and stared at the back of his head, trying to guess how he felt about it.

Ishtar considered his request. 'What would killing him achieve?'

'My sister would be safe. She lives in a city north of the mountains, in a good, solid house, not a hut. She would have his money, enough to look after herself and her daughter.' Pa hesitated, swallowed. 'I do not know if she means it . . . if she would do it . . . but she tells me she would use his money to take in other women who need to escape. That house has many rooms . . .'

The Bone Woman dipped her hands into the sunlit water and wet her brow. She leant forward and stared hard into his eyes, narrowing her own. In that moment, she seemed more like a monster than before, her entire body tensed and poised to strike. Power radiated from her with such intensity I began to feel dizzy. A low buzz throbbed in my ears. I have no idea how Pa managed to remain still and upright, receiving the full force of her glare.

'Are you not just wanting to kill this man to take his wealth for yourself? Once he dies, your laws dictate that you have a right to her money too, do they not?'

Pa struggled to push the words out, his hands balled into fists. 'I know it . . . but . . . I have . . . not . . . considered it,' he said finally. 'I want . . . her . . . to live.'

Ishtar reached out to grasp his chin, tilting his head

back and forth. She looked at him for a long time – at least, it felt that way. My head pounded, and Pa swayed under her gaze. And then finally, she let him go, and Pa exhaled a shaky breath, clutching his temples.

Ishtar seemed unbothered by his discomfort. She thrust the belt buckle back towards him. 'Keep it. You will pay me once I have taken his life.' She stood abruptly, and our time with her was over.

As we turned to leave, I knew this was my only chance. I had been preparing the speech I would give, the questions I would ask, for days, but in her presence I felt my throat dry up and my tongue lie fat and awkward in my mouth. 'What should we call the Goddess, if we kneel at Her feet?' I remember blurting out.

With a strangled-sounding voice, Pa started to apologise and tried to shield my body with his own, but Ishtar waved him off, seemingly pleased by my question. 'Her name is most beautiful. We call Her She Who Swallowed a Universe, because all creation, all life, flows from Her mouth.' She looked at me for a long moment, and I suddenly feared she could see right through my clothing, into my head, and might strike me down for my plans. But she merely said, 'You would do well if you chose to kneel.'

The instant we left the compound, Pa smacked the back of my head. 'Why would you ask that? That religion only accepts women, so don't go getting any ideas.'

But ideas were all I had.

By the time we made our way back, the sun was low

in the sky. Ma greeted us at the doorway, her hands twisted in the folds of her dress. 'Is it done?'

Pa nodded, and she reached out to touch his cheek as he passed, then kissed me on my forehead. 'We waited for you both for the night-meal, come.'

We spoke little that evening. Pa was consumed by his own thoughts and Ma's worry had seeped into the food, making it hard to swallow. Only Tema pretended to be unaffected, scooping up rice from my plate when she saw it was untouched. I tried to preserve this image of them as best I could, feeling like I was being torn in two. I believe that when I left, a small part of me stayed there with them, at that table.

I could not calm myself enough to sleep, my limbs too tense with anticipation. At first light, I crept out of my hut as Ma and Pa slept, carrying just a goatskin of water and my hunting knife. There on the ground, by the doorway, was Tema's green wrap skirt, neatly folded, and the strand of leather she had worn around her neck since she was a baby, coiled like a snake on top of it. That was the only moment my resolve wavered, as I knelt down and held her two most precious possessions in my hands. I thought about what it would mean to leave her behind.

In the end, though, I did not stay. The only part of that morning I regret is that I did not say goodbye. I did not know how to explain my choice to them, or if I would be back, and so I left nothing, not even a note.

It was still cold, but the earth would soon be scorching, so I left my furs at home and ran as much of the way as I could. Without Pa it was easier. The camp was little more than an hour away, and there was nobody else in sight – not even as I approached the entrance. I remember planting each foot into the sand and puffing my chest out, practising how I might walk in there. At the last minute I tied Tema's leather strap around my neck, pulled her skirt off my shoulders and wore it the right way, hoping it would give me strength. I kept my chest bare. A single Woman stood on guard there, holding a scythe with a handle made out of what I hoped was animal bone. She looked down at me, taking in my sweat-covered face, and stared at me for a long time. So long, in fact, that I began to shake, wondering if it was all over. When I tried to explain – to find the words – she simply shook her head and held out her hand for my knife, which I surrendered quickly. She waved me through, and if I had had the courage to look her in the eye – if I had been paying attention to the way she looked at me – I might have felt more at ease.

The sun had fully risen by then, and most of the tents were half-open, but I kept my eyes fixed ahead. The fear of being at the receiving end of their wrath was too great, so I kept my eyes downcast and murmured apologies to any of the warriors I bumped into. Some of them were entirely naked, which made me panic and fix my gaze on the ground in an effort to show them I was being respectful, even though I was desperately curious to look. I needn't have bothered; they barely paid me any attention. It surprised me then, but I know

now how little affects the Bone Women, and how proud they are of their painted bodies. It is a glorious feeling.

When I reached the middle of the compound, I discovered I wasn't the first to have arrived. I wasn't even the second. Four other girls, who must have been no older than fourteen, were already kneeling in front of the great fire, their bodies trembling with exhaustion. I crouched down beside them and pressed my forehead to the warm sand, sweat crawling down my neck. I tried not to panic. To this day I do not know if I fell asleep or if I simply drifted into a state so calm, I left my own body for a little while. I only remember being woken by a Bone Woman as she nudged me roughly with her bare foot.

'What are you doing here?'

I scrambled to my feet, coughing as I accidentally inhaled some of the sand stuck to my lips. She was so tall that I only came up to her chest. Two large, curved daggers were strapped to her hips. I had again rehearsed what I would say on the journey, but it was like a hole opened up in my head and all the words had leaked out. My mouth dusty, I could only gape at her foolishly, until she jerked her head towards the goatskin at my feet.

'Drink,' she ordered. I drank. Half the water missed my mouth and spilled down the front of my tunic. I'm sure she thought I was a fool.

The Bone Woman had fresh tattoos on her cheekbones – she had recently killed. She looked half-dead and half-alive. The other girls had vanished; I wondered if they had been accepted, and the woman had saved my death for last.

'I said – what are you doing here?'

'I . . . I came to kneel. To serve.' I don't know what compelled me to say what I said next. I'd like to think it was being in front of the fire, the source of our power and devotion, that did it. But I think I was simply bursting with the desire to say it. Desperation makes you abandon sense – and carefully prepared speeches – sometimes. 'I know what you are thinking—'

'Do you, now?' She seemed amused by this, so I ploughed on.

'But you see, I am . . . not a boy. Even if I appear as one.'

She examined me without any hint of anger or surprise, and it gave me the courage I needed to continue.

'The gods must have been playing a cruel joke when they pushed me out in this body, dooming me to a lifetime of unbelonging. That – that – is why I am here. I have heard you follow a different doctrine . . .' I remember then that I trailed off, overcome. The words were stuck in my throat and I could no longer speak. My fate was in her hands.

The Bone Woman's eyes travelled down from the top of my shaved head to my feet in their dusty sandals, and to my horror, I began to sob in a loud, ugly kind of way. I was sure she'd walk away from me, disgusted by my tears, or decide I was lying and slice my kidneys out for it. Instead, she laid an inky hand on my shoulder and gripped it tightly. Just like Pa, the day before. 'What do you go by, child?'

'Micah,' I whispered as the tears rolled down my cheeks, and looked directly into her eyes – a bright blue that was rare for these parts.

I think she may have smiled at me. I remember teeth, but fear trumps memory, and it may have just been the tattoos. Nevertheless, what she said went right to the core of me. I carry the words with me today, still.

'I see you now, Micah. Welcome.'

In the days and years that followed, I repeated her words over and over like a mantra. *I see you. Welcome. I see you. Welcome. I see you. I see you.*

Bastet

(EXTRACTS FROM *Stories to Tell Your Five-Year-Old*)

Don't make the mistake of thinking me kind just because I have a womb. A womb is a brutal and bloody land. Glorious.

I am the lion-woman, who sprang forth the moment the sun first touched the earth. Some of you worship me to this day – as you should – but I deserve much more. Let today be your first and only warning.

The stories about me are all true: *keeper of secrets, goddess of fire, devourer of pleasure, the ember escaping from the heart.* I have so many victories under my skin I no longer bother to count them. I breathe life into the mundanity of war; that is why it irks me that so many of you have forgotten how I slayed the chaos god of the underworld – a creature particularly fond of devouring you little things, with your short and silly lives.

I killed him not by beating my chest and howling my intentions at him, but with cunning. I waited until he slept and then crept into his serpent mouth and clawed him to death from the inside, lapping up his blood to quench my thirst.

Shamefully, even fewer of you remember my other

gift to you. You wear it on your ears, your hands and around your neck, but rarely attribute it to me. That changes now.

The first time it happened was delicious. This was in the earlier days when monsters didn't take your small, two-legged forms, and I padded across the earth with a body big enough to plunge an entire country into darkness. Lined with fur, I thought at first I was walking through a thunderstorm. But no, the blood rolled down my legs slowly, slowly at first, almost black, as my womb opened herself, stretching and undulating and pushing impatiently up against me, demanding a response. I stopped, became statuesque for many hours, and watched the red rivers splinter as they slithered through my fur towards the ground. When the milk of me finally splattered on to the land, it hardened and calcified into the glowing green and blue stones which now adorn your bodies. I am the mother of turquoise, a gem rarer than diamonds. Copper and aluminium, a touchstone between my world and yours. You should be thanking me, really. Many of us bleed, but how rare and sweet it is to see a woman reach into the mouth of the world and draw out something imbued with power.

You must be careful with stones so precious. They have a tendency to fester; shrinking around the neck and poisoning the land, should you forget their origins.

Bastet, cattish and poised to jump

Deep Heat

Jiya felt guilty as soon as her phone rang. All three of Jackie's texts remained unopened.

'So . . . are you coming, then?'

No hello. Jackie was hurt.

'Coming . . . where?'

Her friend's sigh over the speaker sounded like she'd tossed the phone on to her bed. 'Jiya. Not again. You promised you'd show up this time.'

Jiya turned to the mirror hooked over the back of her door. She was standing naked in the middle of her bedroom, her underwear balled into her hand. 'Sorry, sorry! Remind me . . . ?'

'Last week on the phone? You said you'd make the next night out, and I've booked us a table at Spinach. Jessica's coming, Amara, Laura, and like . . . everyone else.'

'Spinach? Is that, like, a vegan restaurant or something?'

'Ha. Ha. You KNOW it's a club. We've been wanting to go there for months.'

'Right,' she mumbled, distracted by an ingrown hair on her thigh. 'I'm really sorry. I just forget. I know I've been so shit since—'

'It's fine, don't worry about it,' Jackie said quickly. 'But you keep saying you want to leave the apartment so . . . what about tonight? Can I persuade you? This place is *gooood*, I swear. No house music! We were going to do karaoke first!'

Jiya let the phone drop to her side and glanced around her bedroom, as if a plausible excuse might be propped up in the corner. 'Jackie, you know I love you so much.'

Another sigh. 'So it's a no, then?'

'I . . . I, er, have drawing class at seven, I'm always wiped out after those.' A lie.

'Lisa still keeping you occupied, huh?'

'I haven't really thought about her.' Another lie. 'I should be making more of an effort, I know I should. But I think I'll just drink too much and then make a bad decision.'

'That's okay too, though.' Her friend slowed down a little and did that softening thing with her voice that Jiya always hated. 'I've been here for bad-decision Jiya since preschool!'

'I know, I know. Thank you. But I can barely keep my eyes open.'

The truth was that she couldn't stomach the idea of standing in a loud room, pretending to be a less neurotic version of herself to strangers who were probably doing the same thing back. These days, every time she drank it was like she fell out of her own brain to watch her body do and say things that she didn't truly want it to. The thought of bringing a man or a woman that she hadn't seen in the light of day back to her cramped, ferociously treasured apartment nauseated her.

Plus, it had been a shitty day. The mundane kind of shitty day where she'd stared at the screen and forced herself to tinker about with this week's project, adding in the latest round of revisions. She'd been slow with it, even though Avi had emailed her twice to remind her that the clients wanted the work sooner, rather than later. The problem was that the design was *fine*. But it wasn't amazing, and a part of her still cared. Her mother would have been alarmed at this flatter, sepia-toned version of Jiya, had she been around to see it.

Because it was like Jiya had died a little bit too, it really was. Her friends denied it but Jiya could see it in the gradual but steady decline in her work, in the increasing reliance on patterns and colour combinations she'd developed almost a decade ago. She could feel it, too, in the way she hid herself and avoided being looked at, when she'd have once moved with the ease of someone who doesn't think much about her body at all. She knew this shift had been happening well before death had forced itself into her life, but then April had come and things calcified. And now there was no return; Jiya was certain.

She wanted nothing more than to pour herself a huge glass of wine and sink into her foamy bathtub in her tiny bathroom crammed with candles. There was a time when she did this often, lounging around and chain-smoking with the long jade-green cigarette holder she'd bought as a pretentious seventeen-year-old. And yet – wine gave her a headache, and now the only candle she owned was a single, half-used, vanilla-scented one she'd got from the convenience store round the corner. And Jiya had promised her mother she'd never touch tobacco again after the emphysema diagnosis. You don't break promises you've made to a dead person. Especially not to the person you've shared a bed with for three years. Jiya had fallen asleep every night to the steady hiss and suck of the oxygen tank keeping her small, unyielding mother alive as her lungs shrivelled up like walnuts.

Now, she jammed a joint – pure – into the corner of her mouth instead, and sat at the far edge of the tub, her knees up to her chest as it filled with hot water, close to boiling. A bottle of sparkling, lychee-flavoured water sat on the floor, condensation pooling underneath. Next to it lay a packet of freeze-dried strawberries, untouched. Jiya smoked the first joint quickly, watching ash fall into the water and swirl across her breasts. But the second was a slower affair. She'd take a few puffs then stub it out on the ceramic bath edge for a little while, before lighting up again. Her skin was soft – a little doughy, she felt – and she berated herself for not working out, for not taking better care of herself like her mother had asked her to. She liked her body, but six months ago her gym membership had lapsed and she had refused to renew it when the woman at the desk, blonde and about her age, had called her a cheap *you-know-what* under her breath when Jiya had questioned the sudden price rise. In shock, Jiya had asked to speak to the manager, and when the woman told her she *was* the manager, Jiya said, 'I'm not even Pakistani, you bitch.' And left, so the woman wouldn't see the tears. She still wished she'd come up with something better, agonised over the fact that her reply made it sound like being mistaken for Pakistani was the part she took offence at, not the racism. Many things bothered her about that incident. The fact that 'bitch' seemed like such a tame insult, such a pathetic response. The fact that it happened in the only fucking gym within walking distance. The fact that maybe she *was* Pakistani. Jiya had no idea, because her Guyanese mother had never told her who else had taken part in creating her, only that he had no idea of her existence. And now Jiya would never know him anyway.

As her phone cycled its way through Prince's greatest hits – taste left over from an old relationship – she leant back and absent-mindedly fondled the tap with her foot, her head deliciously heavy. She was thinking about the drawing classes. Missing this evening had rounded up the total number of weekly classes she'd missed to a neat eight. She'd started them half-heartedly in an effort to infuse a bit more life into her graphic design, and since Avi had mentioned in a team meeting that it had worked for him, she'd impulsively bought a six-month course. So far, though, all the classes had done was make her feel incompetent.

It wasn't until her playlist ended that she first heard the muffled, high-pitched whine. Like off-key singing. At first, Jiya assumed it was coming from the pipes, which had always given her and her mother trouble. She pressed her ear to the tile, straining, then followed it down . . . to the water itself.

She tried to ignore the noise for a bit, finishing off the joint and closing her eyes. She slid as far down into the water as she could, bending her knees and submerging herself to just below her nose. Little bubbles formed every time she breathed out. But the whining was persistent and incredibly irritating, and grew louder the closer she got to the water. After a few minutes, Jiya had had enough, cursing as she hauled herself out of the tub and reached for a towel. As she stepped on to the bamboo bathmat, the whine became so loud she froze and looked down at her body, her brain scrambling to fill the gaps.

And that was when she realised the noise was coming from *her*. From between her thighs! She pressed the palm of her hand across the triangle of hair, manoeuvring until the sound visibly decreased. Was she dizzy from the heat of the bath? Hallucinating? A bad joint? A tumour?

'No fucking way!'

Jiya burst into laughter and fell to an awkward squat, her elbow painfully clipping the toilet bowl as she went. The lychee water bottle toppled over and the liquid fizzed onto her toes. 'My . . . clit . . . is . . . singing!' she gasped, clutching the towel to her chest. She was laughing hard, almost maniacally, and yet she could feel sobs rising from her stomach. So it was going to be *that* kind of trip. She closed her eyes and tried to take ten deep breaths. Obviously, she was hallucinating. The joints must've been stronger than she'd realised. She could already picture herself telling the story to her friends, when she finally responded to their texts. She scrunched her toes up, noticing that the sound had stopped. Moving slowly, as if there were an animal in the room with her, she began to towel herself off. And then—

'Where the *fuck* have you been all this time?'

The voice was low-pitched and accusatory – and coming, unmistakably, from between her legs. Jiya froze again and shut her eyes. She was *way* too high. She pressed one palm on to the cold tile and tried to do a grounding technique from one of the YouTube videos she watched whenever insomnia reared its head. *Four things she could touch, three things she could smell—*

'Am I dead?' Jiya said out loud. Her words hung in the air for a moment, and then her clit replied.

'Don't be a fucking idiot.'

It was surreal, at first, to have a conversation with one of her organs. When the high wore off, Jiya's first instinct was to reach for her mother, even though it had been months since her passing at this point. Soledad had never been shocked by anything – she was the kind of unflappable woman who could wake up to find her home on fire and calmly start getting dressed. Jiya had hidden nothing from her, even though the things she wanted and the people she loved had sometimes confused her pragmatic, unsentimental mother. Despite her name, Soledad had never made her feel alone. She would have known what to do. But she was gone, and the shock of it had left her daughter in a constant state of helpless confusion.

Her clit would not stop talking to her. Worse still, it had a personality that reminded Jiya of herself at her least accommodating. Snarky and sarcastic, and constantly demanding attention. It was exhausting.

'At last, you can hear me now, you colossal cunt. Do you know how exhausting it is to whistle for that long?'

'Is this . . . real? Have I just fallen asleep in the tub? Or . . . is this the final stages of a brain tumour? Or – or are you sure I'm not dead?'

'How should I know? You think I'm some omnipresent clit?'

Jiya had pressed her fingers to her closed eyes, rubbing them until little bursts of light filled her vision. Brain tumour. It had to be.

'Do I . . . er. Do you have a name?'

It snorted. 'What do you think?'

'No?'

'I'm a *clitoris*, Jiya. That's my name. Never needed any other.'

'I'm gonna have to give you a name that isn't – I can't – this is already too weird.'

'I won't answer to anything cutesy, so don't fucking try.'

In the end she'd settled on the only name that felt right. Gwyneth.

The first challenge for Jiya had been looking down there to see if anything had changed. The only mirror she owned was fixed above the bathroom basin, so she'd grabbed her phone and flipped the camera, squatting down and squinting. She wondered if she should take a pair of clippers and shave everything off, in case a face was revealed.

'Say something.'

'I fucking won't, thanks.' Gwyneth quivered a little when she spoke, but that was kind of it. Jiya couldn't make out a face, or even a mouth. Her clit looked like it always did. Half-hidden, a little fleshy and mauve.

To her surprise, the adjustment period was brief. Gwyneth clearly understood the inconvenience of the situation for them both. She had no idea how it had happened either.

'I don't know what to tell you,' she would snap when Jiya questioned her, 'I've always been able to speak. You're the one that's started to listen.'

Jiya could only really hear Gwyneth when she was out in the open. As soon as she pulled on underwear, trousers – especially jeans – Gwyneth was silent, which was a huge relief. Big chunks of her day were spent online in meetings with her creative agency, with a mic so sensitive it picked up every creak of her chair. But outside of work, she was shocked to discover her clit was *funny*, often making her laugh in joyful bursts with acerbic observations and a refusal to pity her. Gwyneth mocked her for everything, from the clothes she wore to the shows she binge-watched.

After work, in the heat of the summer evening, Jiya would turn all the lights off and prop open the balcony door, pulling off most of her clothes and settling into the sofa with her legs spread apart for Gwyneth to see properly. She'd smoke and watch the same kind of content that kept her brain quiet: reality TV, rom-coms, celebrity talk shows. Gwyneth would inevitably talk through them all, asking questions, criticising the actors' decisions, laughing hysterically at any earnest declarations of love. She often complained about the view.

'I can barely see! Can't you shave a bit better, for god's sake? Tilt your pelvis up a little? Prop a cushion under there?'

Jiya's lack of flexibility astounded her. She started to take yoga classes and surprised herself by looking forward to them. When she got her period – which had always been messy and irregular – she considered free bleeding to keep the lines of communication open. But Gwyneth surged between sleepy, furious and outrageously sexual, and it became too much of an inconvenience.

A big part of Jiya wondered if she'd finally drifted into the manic depression she'd often feared would come for her. She imagined a doctor mouthing *pushed over the edge* to a co-worker, creeping up behind her with a straitjacket, if she were to go in asking for help. She could picture the conversation: *I woke up one morning and noticed that Mom's hand was gripped around my wrist. And I turned to her and said, 'You okay, Mom?' and she never replied. We shared a bed, and I was always there when she needed me, but this time I didn't wake up and she died holding on to me, asking me to help her, and I didn't. She was still warm. Oh, and I'm the saddest and loneliest I've ever been. So lonely, in fact, that my clit has started talking to me, and I've given it a name and a gender, and I think she might be my closest friend.*

They'd never let her walk out of there.

So, she didn't ask for help. But she did start texting her friends back. She typed out messages like, *Haven't cried in four days! Gold star for me!* Then deleted them letter by letter, and asked them how they were instead.

Her friends remained stubbornly, lovingly, present. They invited her to nights out, movies, birthday parties. She pretended to be annoyed, but was actually deeply thankful. When Cleotilde – an old classmate – had opened up her kitchen cupboards and seen only stale bread and instant noodles, her friends started showing up at her door with takeouts. They insisted on sitting on the floor and eating with her, pretending not to watch every mouthful. It wasn't that Jiya had stopped eating, it was that she'd stopped tasting her food. She no longer savoured the salty, oily, duck-fried rice, the tender chicken cooked in vinegar and butter or the spiced noodle soup that she used to make so often for her and Soledad. Instant noodles and bland sandwiches were easy, no thought or creativity required. But Jiya couldn't summon the energy to explain this, so she choked down the curries and pad thais, and hugged her worried friends gratefully at the door when they left. But her friends weren't caustic and crude with her the way Gwyneth was. They padded her with cotton wool until she felt lazy and sluggish. Gwyneth, however, was relentless in her disapproval of Jiya's solitude.

'You're lonely, and passive about it because you've cut yourself off from the world,' she would snap when

Jiya turned down invitations to go out, or refused Gwyneth's urges to speak to strangers she passed in the street. Where her friends stepped back to give her space, Gwyneth elbowed in and seethed at Jiya's apathy. It irritated her, but only because she knew Gwyneth was right to be mad. She felt like someone had taken a giant spoon and gouged out the most insatiable part of herself. The part that was restless and eager to plunge into the lives and arms of other people – that craved sex, warmth and the smell of another body. Only Gwyneth seemed to have retained some semblance of sexuality, although there was an urgent edge to it that made Jiya uncomfortable sometimes. She was unashamedly lewd, sleazy to the point where Jiya squirmed with embarrassment. Her clit sexualised and objectified everyone around her, stripping them of any agency with a hunger Jiya didn't recognise. It bothered her to think there was an insatiable side of her own self that she couldn't access.

One afternoon, at Gwyneth's urging, she left the stuffiness of her apartment to work in a local coffee shop. She had taken a bite of a creamy, flaky pastry, silky apricot jam filling her mouth, when a woman about her age walked in. Jiya was instantly captivated by her. Between her legs, Gwyneth had a frenetic pulse: *yesyesyesyesyes*. The woman was beautiful, but that wasn't why she couldn't bear to look away from her. It was how she carried herself that made her so memorable. She wore a deep plum dress that clung to her body, yellow eyeshadow and white trainers. She had a smattering of freckles across her bronzed skin, and her hair was freshly twisted into Bantu knots. To Jiya, she seemed genuinely comfortable with being vibrant; a far cry from her own style of loose, earthy cottons and linen. There was a stirring in her stomach that she hadn't felt for a long time, the desire to *reach* and *touch*, and she watched the woman order a coffee and leave, trying to work up the courage to speak to her.

At home, though, Gwyneth had been apoplectic.

'What were you thinking?' she shouted. 'I should be being rubbed to oblivion right now instead of going to bed untouched, *yet again*! Why are you so shit at recognising what you need? What *I* need?'

Jiya had argued back. 'What am I supposed to do? How can I get naked in front of anyone else with you sounding off?'

'I'd be quiet, *obviously*, as you fucked. You think I have no self-control?'

It was one of the few times Jiya disengaged completely, pulling on two pairs of leggings and hugging a pillow as she lay on the sofa and watched a documentary about swingers. Gwyneth would have loved it.

At her clitoris's insistence, Jiya kept trying things. Just to shut her up, of course. Turkish eggs topped with sumac and chilli oil, instead of plain toast for breakfast. Morning walks to buy fancy, creamy coffees. She found a gym that was a little further away but had a pool and started swimming on the weekends. She bought a CityCulture pass and went to more exhibitions, even if she could only concentrate on them for half an hour before feeling listless and empty. But most importantly, she went back to life drawing class. For the inspiration, she told Gwyneth. But also for Lisa.

Pre-Gwyneth, Jiya had brought along a box of charcoal and spent the first few weeks ignoring the models altogether, turning her paper into a seething, chalky mass of black. She'd leave the class with her eyes red and charcoal smeared up to her elbows. If Lisa, who had shoulder-length auburn hair and an open smile that made Jiya eager to gain her attention, had concerns about her student, she kept them to herself.

Lisa was the kind of teacher who made everyone feel safe. She murmured suggestions to the students instead of loudly pointing out their mistakes and stayed tactfully silent when she saw teardrops dotting Jiya's work.

When she finally returned to the classes, Jiya expected to move through them in a blur, like before. But Gwyneth made it impossible. Her clit reacted to people and their smells, the clothing they wore and the timbre of their voices. The models were especially open to scrutiny; Jiya caught herself fixating on hairy toes, or dimpled cheeks. She started to get distracted by the way the light caught a head of hair or followed a line of sweat from the nape of a neck to the bottom of a tailbone.

By her sixth class, she was enthralled. Their model for that evening was a man in his mid-forties, with stooped shoulders and a thin nose. His mouth was downcast and permanently pressed shut in a delicate line, which she struggled to replicate with her thick charcoal. His hair was messy, curly, and it trembled as he crouched with his hands resting between his feet, testicles almost skimming the floor. Lisa lit several candles which made his balls cast a shadow that stretched across the ground behind him and swayed whenever he moved. Jiya was mesmerised. She couldn't take her eyes away from him and his thighs, which quivered a little from the strain of holding the pose. She wanted to reach out and tousle his hair – not in a sensual way, but to startle him, to make him look at her.

The class lasted for an hour and a half, but that particular one felt longer. Jiya was so determined to get him right that her hands cramped, and she sagged with relief when Lisa announced that it was time to pack up. She had been so focused on trying to capture the model's energy that she'd shut out the entire world around her – her grief, the loneliness, Gwyneth – all of it melted away as she obsessed over the angle of his knees. Her shoulders were stiff from hovering around her ears, and her neck *ached*. Nevertheless, Jiya was proud of her sketch. It was the first one she bothered to keep, taping it to her wardrobe. Although there was something about the model she found attractive, she didn't want him in that way. Which is why what happened a few nights later was such a surprise.

She woke with a gasp, her heart pounding, entirely naked on her stomach with her hand between her—

'What just happened?'

Gwyneth was laughing thickly, like she was half-asleep. 'Ah, that was great. It's been a while.'

'Did . . . did *you* make me do that?'

'I don't control you at all, Jiya,' her clit said sharply, suddenly sounding wide awake. 'If I did, you'd be attending to me twenty-four seven, because I'm *always* gagging for it. You were dreaming of your little model friend from class, and I was having an exceptional time. There's no shame in it.'

'I'm not ashamed.' Jiya flipped on to her back and wondered if she could be bothered to get up and wash her hands. 'I just haven't felt the urge to do that in forever.'

'Feels good, though, doesn't it? Who knew that old man could get your gears going!'

She started waking up two, three times a night after that, after orgasming in an explosive burst. It would always set Gwyneth off laughing, or even singing – sluggish, but quick to tell Jiya off for stopping even as the final few waves of pleasure were still making their way through her body.

Jiya had started to feel excited about things again. Excited about seeing Lisa and having her bend over her work to offer a murmured piece of advice, sometimes taking the charcoal from Jiya's hand to demonstrate a technique. She both wanted to impress her and harness the mounting enthusiasm bubbling up inside her chest. She started to imagine Lisa's hand closing over hers, jagged charcoal moving across paper in stuttering little lines – quicker, sharper, harder. Gwyneth would stutter: *yesyesyesyesyes—*

Which is why, after the next art class, Jiya decided she was ready. As people started to pack up, and the model pulled on a chiffon robe, she made her way over to Lisa and blurted out, 'I think I'd like to model next time. I mean, not next time if you've got someone already . . . I just mean, whenever there's a free space.'

'Jiya, that's . . . amazing!' Lisa's eyebrows had vanished into her fringe. 'I had no idea you were interested!' She pulled a small red diary from her pocket, flipped to the back page and glanced up at her.

'We actually do need someone for next week? If you're up for it, of course. You can just sign up on the sheet over there.' There was a little challenge in her voice – as if she expected Jiya to fumble her way out of it – that made her pull the pen from Lisa's outstretched hand and write down her name and number.

By the time she got home, she was covered in sweat and already regretting it. But Gwyneth was *ecstatic*, trilling while Jiya pulled herself into the bathtub and started lathering her hair up with shampoo.

'This is good for us. Really good. Some action at-fucking-last!'

'It's *not* action. You know you're gonna have to stay silent the whole time, don't you? Or I'm backing out. I mean it.'

'Yeah, I know, so you keep saying. I'll shut up, but only because I want you to keep at it. This is a start, you know? First you do a little naked modelling, next you're in a threesome in some rich frat boy's apartment. Or stripping off at sex parties and doing shots out of belly buttons, all that shit. Text Jackie and make her take you to Spinach! If you don't lean into this and

show a little enthusiasm, I am going to be so angry,
Jiya. I'm fed up.'

'I'm not going to a sex party.'

'. . . yet.'

She decided to put a little more effort into her dinner
that evening: marinating tender strips of beef in spiced
coconut milk, and frying up her rice in garlic, nigella
seeds and ghee before she covered it with water. She'd
been keeping plantain in her cupboard for a week,
waiting for them to blacken, and now she pulled out
a couple and fried them, then sprinkled nutmeg and
cinnamon sugar over the top. She ate the thick slices
with her hands, the oil running down between her
knuckles and making her glisten. *Yesyesyesyesyes.*

Palate Cleanser II

You might be inclined to say she committed a murder to save her own life. And she'd be inclined to agree. Now, in the mornings, she presses her forehead to the floor in prayer, but not to God, to herself.

Sweat collects in fat beads at the base of her neck and pools quietly between her breasts; she bears it, she bears it. If the human foot could leave an imprint of the past with every step, hers would be a trail of blood and placenta, still staining the soles of her feet. Two endings before their stories began. Two and counting. Neither welcomed, both mourned. Both created in the eye of a lonely storm with a man who once slammed her into the wall so hard the skin split, wrapped a hand around her throat and squeezed as the other hand pressed between her legs. Moved in a circular motion. And she, body poised and prepared to die, watched him as he told her how he owned her and what he'd do to her if she strayed.

She'd always been afraid of gas stoves. After their small home had exploded with him asleep and drugged, as she watched from the outside, she had accepted everything would be different now. A murderer. A free woman.

No one caught her, after all, and now she is beyond their reach anyway, deep in her life on a new continent, worshipping herself and the moment she picked up a match like a dagger and struck her own life back into existence.

Texas Has a Limit on How Many Dildos You Can Own

But you can own as many guns as you want, so at least there's that. That's what we used to joke about in Shelby's Bar on a Saturday night, back when we were nineteen and still dating whoever would take us – truthfully that was almost anyone. Birth control had been around for a minute, and sex was *all* over the place. You know what a dildo is, young man? How old are you, anyway? Oh really? Same age as my youngest. So you know what a dildo is, then? I'm only asking because who knows what you kids are into these days. And if you don't know what they are, the whole story I'm trying to tell you won't make any kinda sense. Anyway, that's what you get for coming here on a Wednesday afternoon and bothering me for stories about . . . what was it, again?

Oh yeah, Shelby's. But what's a New York paper doing covering a little run-down bar in El Paso? A feature? Why? Shelby's went and shut down about twenty good years ago. She was twenty-five when she inherited that place from her pa. Never changed the name, y'know? That's right, that's right, her old man named it Shelby's – she barely changed a thing.

That was a different time though, y'know? We thought – d'you mind if I smoke? – we thought we were immune to bad things happening. Nowadays, I'd sure as hell never go home with a guy like the one I went home with that night I was telling you about – the one with all the dildos. He was in his thirties, with a soul patch and a delicious, hairy chest. I wanted to bury my face into that chest and breathe in the smell of sweat as we made love – or I guess I would've said 'carried on' in those days. The funniest man, you could just tell he was the kinda guy who knew a little bit about everything, and didn't care what anyone thought of him.

You know, I still think it's odd that you came on over all this way to do a piece on a little old bar that don't run no more. But it was a special place, wasn't it? At least back then. Can I get you a coffee? You'll need to go buy creamer if you want a coffee, I drink it without. I don't know how you New York kids take it. You sure you don't want any? All right, suit yourself. Means I can get back to my story.

His bedroom was something wild, the entire ceiling was made of little reflective tiles, like a giant disco ball had crashed into his ceiling. I loved it, I had no taste! And stranger still, around all four walls he had this long-running shelf – it was only interrupted by the doorframe, but no door, would you believe it? Just one of those tacky beaded curtains. And the shelves were stacked with dildos. I didn't even clock what they were at first, mind you. I hadn't seen any before. But Marcel – that was his name – showed me his collection and explained how you used them. It was real fascinating. There were dildos made of glass, dildos that could be attached to a harness so a woman could wear 'em, dildos that looked so big and fat my own asshole clenched up in fear at the thought. I was a god-fearing woman – sort of – back then. Young and looking for adventure, but still a little shy. I've changed a lot since then – I go to church sometimes. I know you probably think me senile, the way I'm rambling, but it's been a long time since I got to tell this story and I remember it clear as daylight.

Anyway, Marcel showed 'em all off, these rubbery, plasticky things, and some had names, although most didn't. And then he told me he was breaking the law big time, because in Texas there's a limit on how many dildos you can own. Marcel said, if the police ever came to his place and raided it, they'd leave all the guns he had in his truck, under his bed and on his kitchen table where he liked to strip them down and clean 'em. But they'd take his dildos and he'd probably get fined, or arrested – or worse, him being who he was. And I wasn't all that interested in the guns *or* the dildos to tell you the truth, I just wanted to add a cool, older guy like Marcel to the notches of my bedpost. I wanted a story. I grew up right here, did I mention? The seven of us had two bedrooms between us: me, Keely, Ma and Pa, Jackson, Lisa and William. I grew up dirt poor, and I've worked in that leather factory my goddamn entire life, pardon my blasphemy. I thought I was getting out of here when I was nineteen. I thought everything was a lot easier than it really is. I got three, maybe four good years, and then Ma died, and Lisa got sick, and I wound up right back in the place I didn't want to call home. Never went to Shelby's after that. Just didn't feel like I belonged there any more.

To this day – and I been married twice, like I told you – Marcel was one of the craziest, funniest men I've ever been with. He mentioned he was a lawyer, which I thought was pretty funny given how he was breaking the law. But that's why I believed him when he started talkin' about all the dildo stuff. So. I stopped him from talking and said I wanted to see our bodies on that crazy, stupid ceiling of his. And what a gentleman! He didn't try to get any of the dildos involved, and I was grateful at the time – but now I wonder if he thought I was too young and too green for it. I was, but at the time I would have pretended otherwise. And a part of me wishes I'd been a bit braver, y'know? The way you feel when you look back at your younger self, so worried about all this stuff that just *don't matter*, and missin' out on the little moments of life happening right in front of you 'cause you're too busy looking ahead. Yeah, I did that all the time.

Anyway, afterwards, we – the girls and I – joked about it a lot in Shelby's. It came to be one of those things you say again and again in every kind of situation, especially when we got riled up about things like politics and war. We'd talk about the latest front-runner for governor or whoever and joke, 'I bet he's got a whole lot of dildos!' Shelby's was real good for that – cheap beer and cigarettes letting us turn everything into a story, a joke about sex, and a political stance. Nothin' beats being nineteen and having all the time in the world to sit with your thoughts and pass 'em around. There is something glorious about being young and thinking *I'd never accept that shit.* But you know, you get older, and the bills get bigger, and thoughts of progress and civil rights and sexual revolution can only protect you against numbness for so long, I guess. The truth is I barely had time to think about freedom and politics because puttin' food on the table exhausted me enough.

And then y'know, you're feeding your kid, your kids, your grandkids, life has steamrollered away and now I'm an old woman and no one listens to me any more, even you, with your phone and your notebook. You just want me to talk about Shelby's, but you're missing the point about what the place was to us – to me – because you don't want to hear my stories. Never would have given me the time of day if it weren't for your paper. I've never heard of your paper – I don't think they sell it down here. Can you send me a copy when your story comes out? You know, I don't think the laws have changed anyhow, have they? Still can't own more than six – or was it seven? – dildos in Texas but you can carry guns without a licence. Six, you say. Yeah, that sounds about right. I wonder how Marcel is doing these days. Probably dead. I wouldn't mind seeing that chest one more time. He must've owned a lot of guns, Marcel.

Man in a Can!

**PIONEERING START-UP She Knows
Best LAUNCH 'REVOLUTIONARY'
PRODUCT: MAN IN A CAN!**

She Knows Best, the pioneering start-up with ambitious
claims, have today launched a product they believe will
revolutionise domestic labour and even the playing field
for women, *Women Weekly* reports.

Described as an 'innovative product for the new age
of independence' by *Technical Futures*, Man in a Can!
is exactly what it says on the tin – a bespoke, space-
efficient assistant who will take on all the unpleasant
work that you don't feel like doing, but won't give you
all the hassle of a handyman or boyfriend. Or, as the She
Knows Best strapline puts it, 'the guy you need – until
you don't!'

The company claim that Man in a Can! is designed
to fit into the lives of busy working women, justifying
eye-watering prices starting from $58,000 by offering a
lifetime guarantee and promising a pleasant customer
experience 24/7. The description on the She Knows Best
website reads:

No matter what time of day, just pop the lid open, tell him what you want, then sit back and relax as your man crawls out of his tiny tin home and expands to his full height of six feet. He'll complete any household tasks you need, carry your shopping, and even sync to your car and act as a chauffeur! Best of all, he'll learn on the go, remembering how you like your bath, what your favorite flowers are, and even what color to paint your nails! An IRL boyfriend could never!

John Smith, She Knows Best cofounder, said, 'It's 2045. We all know women don't need men to live full, happy lives – as far as trends go, pale, male and stale is finally out! We wanted to create a product that aligns neatly with our company's core value of feminism, choosing exactly how you spend your time and hard-earned money. That's why we have designed the perfect tool to help you live your best life, without needing to take care of anyone else!

'I co-founded She Knows Best with my business partner, Smith Johnson, when I realized how much work it was to run a home, take care of the kids and work full-time. My wife was away for a weekend, and it really opened my eyes to the impossible reality women live with. It's not acceptable – we men *need* to do better. I sat down in my home office that very evening and began brainstorming. Together, Smith and I have spent almost a decade perfecting the technology that we are sure will change women's lives for the better and make up for decades of inequality.'

Indeed, the initial feedback from testers has been overwhelmingly positive. Sarah McKinnon, one of 200 beta users of Man in a Can!, reported, 'Honestly, the thing I love most is how polite they are. I'm so sick of men interrupting me, but Ralph is programmed to serve, and he comes fully dressed in a pale grey suit, navy tie and black shoes – so stylish! I could take him as a date to a wedding – in fact, I just might!

'At first, I wasn't sure what to use him for. But it became obvious fairly quickly – I needed a lightbulb changed, and he did it within minutes. Then it was the funky-smelling drain I hadn't gotten round to unclogging, and then, before I knew it, I was sending him off to deal with my landlord, who has always been a bit inappropriate. Now that I've got Ralph, I wouldn't ever give him up! I just feel like life is too short to spend time doing boring, tedious chores when I could be out there living the life I've always wanted, and smashing the patriarchy!'

One highly unique aspect of the product is its diminutive size, no larger than a tin of sardines. Available in four bespoke colours – pink, raspberry, cream, and glitter – the can has rounded, soft edges so as not to snag on items of clothing or damage freshly manicured nails, and opens at the very simple click of a button. The men themselves are self-assembling nano bots that come pre-programmed based on a detailed online form buyers fill in at checkout. She Knows Best claim this is to enhance the customer experience and ensure women aren't bogged down with unnecessary admin.

'Keeping things user-friendly is key,' explained Head of Product Design, Richard Smithson, when *Women Weekly* reached out with further questions. 'That's why we don't provide user manuals. Women are busy enough! We encourage our customers to sit back, relax and let their men take care of the nonsense.'

The company – who received the majority of funding from the Pentagon in exchange for exclusive access to their IP – have paid special attention to detail when it comes to diversity and inclusion. Man in a Can! is available in over forty different skin tones – a stunning feat for a new company – and comes with hundreds of customizable features. Although the product won't be available nationally until March 31, you can pre-order yours at www.sheknowsbest.com today. Readers of *Women Weekly* get an exclusive 15% discount on advance orders – so run, don't walk!

If that doesn't persuade you, next month She Knows Best are also launching Man in a Can! After Dark 'for all your womanly needs' and Man in a Can! Streamline, which comes in a foldable steel wallet that's perfect for slipping into your tote or purse.

Man in a Can! You *can* do it all, but you shouldn't have to!

End

She Knows Best is not at liberty to discuss IP. Contact Richard Jones: richardjonespr@sheknowsbest.com for further questions.

She Knows Best welcomes any and all questions from Feminists, Women and Women's Groups. Contact John Jones: johnjoneshr@sheknowsbest.com. Replies can take up to 95 working days.

Medusa

(EXTRACTS FROM *Stories to Tell Your Five-Year-Old*)

I've heard it's fashionable to retell what happened to me these days, and reclaim my story as something more than what it was. Famous for being beautiful, famous for being hideous. Punished by a woman for the sins of a man, then killed by a man to protect a woman. The story goes that my head of snakes was cut off and I was turned to stone. It's wrong, but it suits me just fine.

Fascinating, what I've come to represent: that gendered rage, that woman scorned, that victim, so helpless and tearful . . . I've heard the latest version paints me as the maker of my own destiny, far more in control than once thought. I've heard a lot of things, whispered in my ear. *Mortal, god, goddess, monster, killer of man,* or something equally amusing. It's been so long since I've existed as a body of any kind that I can barely remember the loss. No one comes looking for me any more – but you all still talk about me, don't you?

The official story is that I died, which makes me laugh. Dead! At the hands of a little man and his shiny piece of metal! *Please.*

Some of you are closer to the truth than I thought

imaginable. I don't know how you could possibly know I'm still around, but I feel you reaching for me. I feel it in your hot, angry blood – in your veins, your arteries, your capillaries, when I'm in there, racing around in glee.

Medusa. Am I under your skin yet? Am I?

Enough with the jokes about men. Jesus fucking Christ, we get it.

Hospitality

The bar is mostly made of dark and deeply scarred wood, with a sticky sheen that can never quite be wiped away. Behind it are rows of liquor bottles, the glint of their colours – blues, reds, pinks, greens, the occasional yellow – illuminated by soft lighting above them. The owner, often absent, built these shelves himself and is extremely proud of his handiwork. He instructs the staff to dust the bottles twice a day, and always checks that the labels are facing the customers. The bar is high too. It's designed to prevent anyone from jumping over the counters, where they would smash into neatly stacked, polished glasses of all shapes and sizes; the most delicate of all, of course, being the dusty champagne flutes.

The most important thing about this bar is that there is only one way in and out: a narrow entrance about half a metre wide. It is easy to trap someone in there, for example, and make them think they are going to die a sudden and brutal death. But of course, no one thinks about this when designing restaurants or installing dark wooden panels in a rectangle, with a solitary, narrow exit.

The assistant manager *does* think about this, though. Very occasionally, she finds herself launched into some profoundly disturbing thoughts. They explode into her brain, landmines with mysterious triggers. It's not that she *wants* to think about the ways she could die, but there have been moments in her life when she thought she might, and those cannot be forgotten. One particular moment has grown roots deep into the muscles of her shoulders, leaving them hard and lumpy like an old mattress. That moment had—

'How's it going?'

The assistant manager glances up with a sheepish jolt. She's been doing it again. It's easier when the shifts are quiet, like this Monday night. She smiles automatically and moves to the beer taps, guessing the man standing in front of her (mildly attractive, slim-built, probably privately educated) will go for a beer. A Kronenbourg 1664 maybe, or the Amstel.

'A pint of the 1664 for Matthew, please.'

She dislikes the way he refers to himself in the third person, like she's a child. It brings to mind the mothers and fathers at the park, or on the Tube, saying things like, 'Mummy is very tired, so please use your inside voices.' Or, 'Just a moment, Daddy is on a phone call.'

'Coming right up!' she chirps.

Matthew is appraising her as if he's about to ask her something she won't want to answer, his eyes sweeping over her hair and facial features. Calculating. She knows what's coming. Fixes her gaze to the pint she's pouring.

Matthew (expensive suit, wedding ring front and centre) waits until she's holding the card machine out to him, reluctantly dependent on the speed with which he pays for his drink. He doesn't move.

'Where are you from?' he asks her, his finger hovering above the keypad. The assistant manager feels irritation needling her skin.

'Here.'

'Sure but . . . where are you *from*? Where are your parents from?'

'South London.' She nudges the card machine closer so it's touching his fingers, and he takes it from her and starts to enter his PIN.

'You look Hispanic. Or Italian. Or . . .' Matthew brightens suddenly. 'Wait, are you Persian?' He says the word strangely, drawing the 'er' out so it sounds like he's saying 'purrr-shan'. The card machine spits out a receipt and the assistant manager whips it away from him, concentrating on neatly tearing the paper and handing the customer his card back. She smiles tightly and repeats, 'London.'

She senses he's going to ask *again*, so turns to her co-worker who is hovering by the coffee machine, helpless. It's only the girl's second shift, but her lack of proactivity isn't a promising sign.

The assistant manager busies herself re-explaining the knobs and dials to the new girl before making a latte. She takes care to show her how to make a perfect foam from cold milk, hoping that it will soon become one less task to worry about.

When the assistant manager turns back to the bar, Matthew is mercifully gone, pint drained and empty on the sticky surface. Two customers now stand in front of her. Ian (balding, barrel-like, a tenner clamped in his fist) who she recognises from last summer, when England made it to the World Cup finals and her boss had installed two TVs for the customers. He orders two pints and then takes them to drink alone outside, smoking under a heater. And then there's the American. She recognises the woman (brunette, bejewelled, maybe mid-forties) standing opposite her now as someone she'd refused service to the previous night. The woman had been too drunk to serve, stumbling through the pub doors from the hotel across the road. There had been such obvious desperation in her wobbly footsteps last night, it made the assistant manager want to avoid her, as if she were a black hole of misery who risked sucking in those who came too close. Nevertheless, she smiles and is relieved when the woman fleetingly smiles back.

'Good evening – Kay, was it?' the assistant manager says warmly. 'What can I get you?'

'I'll have a whisky – you don't have Corsair, do you? No? Okay, I guess . . . I guess I'll take the Daniel's then, honey. Double shot on the rocks, please. And can I have four ice cubes? Everyone in this city serves me with one or two, and I just don't understand it.'

The assistant manager turns around to scan the shelves for the Jack Daniel's.

'Listen, honey, how old are you? Old enough to be serving me?' The woman (small mouth, dyed red hair, impeccable teeth) peers at her, a little suspiciously. The assistant manager, busy making sure there are exactly four ice cubes in her highball, tries to pinpoint her accent but she can only distinguish between the twang of the deep south or the classic nasal of the valley girl, and the woman's voice sounds like neither.

'Honey?' The boldness in Kay's voice is grating. As if her opinion and hers alone is the standard by which everything around her operates.

'I'm twenty, Kay. So, old enough!' Smiling, the assistant manager hands her the receipt and gently pushes the glass towards her, hoping she'll choose to sit somewhere other than the bar.

'That's a little young to be serving, isn't it?'

'The legal drinking age here is eighteen.'

Kay (mascara a little smeared, fingernails picking at the hem of her silk blouse) doesn't remember having this conversation the previous night, because she'd been completely hammered. She is new here but carries the same air of familiarity as many of the regulars; someone who is quietly fading. Lonely. Alone.

'That seems so young! Where I'm from you need to be twenty-one and over to be behind the bar, and rightly so, I think.' Kay rotates the highball between slim, manicured fingers and continues, 'I'm no Mormon, I promise you that, but I do think young girls shouldn't be working in places like *this*.'

She gestures vaguely to the bottles of liquor behind the assistant manager, exaggerating the movement. 'Why aren't you in school?'

'I *am*. I'm a uni student.' The assistant manager doesn't want to have this conversation again. She speaks quickly and flatly, as if reading from a script. 'Forensic Criminology. I work here because I live above the bar.' *And because the owner gives me the cheapest rent I could find, in exchange for closing up. It's not like I'm here for the laughs, Kay.*

Kay sighs and shakes her head.

'Oh, honey.' She pauses to sip from her glass. 'I'm glad to see you're so responsible for someone your age but I really don't think this is the place for you.' On this, they both agree.

Kay points to a jar of mixed nuts. 'Those complimentary?'

'It's £3.95 for a bowl.'

'Lord, you Brits are cheap. I'll take one.'

The assistant manager turns to her colleague, intending to suggest she give it a go. It's a simple task, not really one she could fuck up. But the girl has vanished – probably in the bathroom on her phone. She sighs and places the bowl between them. 'Do you want to pay now, or start a tab?'

Kay digs into the nuts and ignores her question. 'I'm here for a conference, for work. I'm the Head of Sales for Sherman's – well, interim Head of Sales, but I'm just an interview away from the official title. I've only been at the company for a couple of years, you know, so it's a pretty impressive rise. I've got a ten-year plan now, that involves me making it to managing director and buying myself a nice big ranch house, maybe a coupla horses. Do you know Sherman's?'

'No.'

'We're a construction company, fifty years strong.

International clients – we've probably built a good chunk of your office buildings. Like I said, I've only been there a few years, but this could really be it for me. We're like a family.' She speaks quickly and loudly, even though the assistant manager is barely a metre away from her. She raps the bar with her knuckles. 'I'll have another.'

As the assistant manager piles a fresh highball with ice, the new hire slips back into the bar. She's intercepted before she can slink away to pretend to clean the coffee machine.

'I need you to check the tables outside,' the assistant manager snaps. 'Collect the glasses and empty out ashtrays – and table 26 is looking like they'll want another round. So check them too, please.'

'It's cold outside,' the girl says slowly, as if she's speaking to an idiot. The assistant manager grabs a tray and holds it out to her.

'Then wear your coat.'

Kay watches this interaction with interest, resting her head on her hand. 'You know,' she says conspiratorially, as the girl slouches away, tray tucked under her arm, 'I find that positive reinforcement is best when it comes to leadership.'

The assistant manager holds her breath for a moment, fighting the urge to tell Kay that leadership is the last thing on her mind; all she wants to do is get through her shift and then get into her bed, in her cold room with the window that rattles in the wind and leaks when it rains.

'I'll bear that in mind.'

The new girl comes back with a trayful of empty glasses. 'That bald guy outside wants another.' She hands the assistant manager a pile of coins. 'He said to keep the change.'

The assistant manager holds back from saying, *Another what? You have to ask what it is he wants!* She knows Kay's watching, and she also remembers that Ian is a Moretti man. But the girl's incompetence only irritates her further. She'd almost rather work alone than work with people who force her to explain the obvious.

Kay slurps loudly at the melting ice in her drink, her face a little pink, and the assistant manager picks up a tray, mostly to get away from her. When she sticks her head outside, she sees the new girl didn't bother to collect the overflowing ashtrays. As she passes Ian, scrolling on his phone, she picks up his glass. 'One more, right?'

He doesn't look up. 'I'll come and have it inside.'

As soon as the assistant manager repositions herself behind the bar, Kay raises her empty glass in the air. 'I'd like another, please.' She slides over a fifty. 'You can keep the change.'

'Thanks, Kay.'

The tip is just over a fiver, which, to be fair, is more than most people give. Although it's not enough to pull her out of her bad mood, the assistant manager feels herself softened slightly by pity. This is the part of the job she finds the hardest: the way people unload their baggage on to her and then expect her to smile and be grateful for the pennies they leave behind. It never occurs to them that perhaps *they* are the source of her discomfort.

Working behind a bar, she's learnt there are two kinds of loneliness. The first one makes people withdraw; they barely speak, they sit drinking alone and watch life unfold around them. This type of lonely people were mostly men who left her alone, easier for her to deal with than the second type, like Kay. Kay is a moth, drawn to the light of others and looking for someone to talk at until last orders; not seeing her as a real person but as a warm, shiny reflection, pinned down by the requirements of her job. Kay is going to give her trouble, she's certain. The demands for her time, the heavy drinking, the unsolicited advice, she just knows this woman is going to draw her Monday night out as long as she possibly can.

'Just so you're aware, the kitchen closes at nine.'

'I don't eat after six.' Kay winks at her. 'Keeps the tush and the tum in check.'

A few minutes pass in silence. Then Kay suddenly drains her entire glass and says loudly, 'Honey, you're so lucky. You have your whole life ahead of you! What are you *doing* here?'

To the assistant manager's horror, Kay bursts into loud sobs and reaches across the counter, clutching for her right hand.

The assistant manager snatches her hand back and asks, rather limply, 'Um. Are you all right?'

'You don't know how hard it is.' Kay gasps at her like a dying fish, her eyes unfocused. 'You're so *young*.'

The assistant manager is exhausted and behind on

her reading for her seminar tomorrow. She'd hoped that she'd be able to catch up on it tonight, but that plan is quickly circling the drain. She hasn't got the bandwidth to be engulfed by Kay's sadness right now.

'I . . .' She spots Ian (stocky, bald; perhaps, from the paint on his clothes, a builder?) walking in from the cold. In her haste to extricate herself from Kay's wailing, she doesn't see the stagger in his walk. 'I'm so sorry, Kay, I need to serve this customer.'

'I need another drink!' Kay demands, and the assistant manager assures her she'll be right with her. She wishes, yet again, that her new colleague could pour a decent pint. But she seems reluctant to improve at anything that involves interacting with other people, which the assistant manager resents.

Ian (dirty shoes, small black backpack clenched in one fist) is leaning on the bar and peering at the beer taps with a slight squint. He barely glances at her, but nods when she hands him a pint topped with a perfect ring of foam.

'You from around here, love?'

At first the assistant manager assumes Ian's talking to her, but it's Kay he's turned towards. She's gripping her glass with both hands and says, stiffly, 'I'm from Provo.'

'Where's that, then? California?'

Kay glances at the assistant manager and then back at Ian, disgust scrawled across her pinched face. 'Provo is in *Utah*.'

'Oh, is it now?' Eyebrows raised mockingly, Ian smirks into his pint as he picks it up. He's swaying slightly and it is then the assistant manager realises that he is already drunk. Too drunk. Possibly verging on belligerent. She should have refused him service. The realisation hits her wetly, like a blood spatter, and she suddenly wishes she was far away from him. Unease settles into her bones as she watches him take a gulp of the beer, almost cradling it in his hand.

Ian (bloodied lip, short fingernails) is a dangerous thing, although no one finds this out until half an hour later. He's also a father. He brings out an iPhone with a shattered screen displaying a picture of two young boys, and tells her about Luke and John – five and seven, beaming up at her. It's the first time he's really noticed her all evening, and she can feel the focus of his gaze like a laser now, charging the air around them. The assistant manager usually prides herself on being rational and calm, but there is something about Ian that makes her want to crouch down behind the bar, stuff her fingers in her ears and close her eyes until he leaves.

Ian asks if he can charge up his phone. He's just there for one last quick one, he tells her, and then he'll be on his way, but he needs a decent charge to get home. The assistant manager plugs the phone into her own charger, almost tiptoeing with anxiety. She doesn't want to talk to him but he won't drink quietly, or quickly. He's standing in the narrow gap of the bar entrance, and therefore he is between her and the only way out. Ian's decision to stand there has created an unavoidable shift, and when the assistant manager speaks, her voice is not really her own. She understands why he has chosen that spot – it's close to his phone – but she wishes he would choose somewhere, anywhere else to stand.

She nods and smiles as he talks at her, folding herself inwards and inching over to where Kay is still waiting, now tapping a sleek American Express impatiently on the dark, scarred wood. As soon as Ian's attention wanes, the assistant manager is apologising to Kay and asking her what she can get her. Things have shifted between them, too. She is hoping for an ally, but Kay is annoyed by Ian's presence sucking up all the oxygen in the room. Kay does not like the feeling of being ignored. She spits out her order and makes a point of tipping a single pound this time, then removes herself to a low table, her back to the bar. The assistant manager notes Kay has now had four double whiskies and should probably not be given any more and lets herself relax a little against the chill of the soft-drinks fridge. Perhaps this fear is nothing more than the sensation already living in her shoulders, creeping up to her neck. Perhaps.

But when she looks up again, Ian is staring at her. He is still, the fresh beer next to him, taking in her body in a way that makes her feel pinned down and confused. When at last she meets his eye, Ian makes a licking motion with his tongue at her, so fast she almost misses it. She freezes and he grins, like they've both shared a private joke. Later, she will wonder if this was the tipping point.

It is becoming clear that Ian has no intention of leaving soon. The assistant manager watches him wander around the small pub with its dark and deeply scarred wooden panelling and feels glued to the ground, her fingers twitching. She pulls the new girl back into the bar and tells her to stay close. Ian appears to be on a rolling, tilting, swaying ship. Like a toddler fighting sleep, he pitches backwards and forwards, one fist tightly clenched around the black backpack, the other around the pint, barely touched. Some of it has slopped on to the floor.

The assistant manager watches as he irritates a young couple, pulling a chair up to their table. They make polite conversation with him, the woman smiling, although the shadows of the candle in front of her make it seem like she's crying. The man has an arm on the woman's knee, making sure Ian sees it. The assistant manager wants to intervene and apologise, she wants to hand Ian back his phone and tell him to leave. But that moment between them earlier, the slither of his tongue, the enjoyment of her discomfort, keeps her standing still. Ian has brought something inky and malleable in the door with him that she can't articulate. She can feel it in the way he uses his whole body to impose himself on other people, his assumption that everyone needs to know about him and his two young boys, the way he looks at her like she exists just for him. She can see that the woman opposite Ian is frozen too, her shoulders tensed up by her ears. The assistant manager watches her shake her head, slowly. A few metres away, in a small alcove by the door, Kay sits, now crying quietly again. Her sadness spills across the table. Occasionally, she glances at Ian with distaste on her face.

As the assistant manager prepares to approach Ian and quietly offer him a glass of water, he lurches to his feet mid-sentence, without any warning. They watch him stagger too far to the right as he abandons his drink and heads towards Kay. It's as if his body is only just realising how truly drunk he is, when he drapes himself on the alcove, leaning heavily against a wooden beam. He says something to Kay that she doesn't like, and she hesitates for a moment, and then as Ian looks back to his forgotten pint she darts out of her seat and approaches the bar like a storm, her blow-dry practically crackling from nervous electricity.

'Listen, honey,' Kay says the second she reaches the bar, 'you need to make him leave. He's bothering me. I have the right to drink in peace.'

The assistant manager knows Kay is right, but in that moment anger pulsates through her and she wishes the woman in front of her would just keep quiet and endure it, the same way she herself has. This shouldn't be her fucking problem to deal with and she resents Kay for offloading it on to her.

'I know. I'm so sorry.' But it's herself the assistant manager is apologising to, for all of it. For putting herself in this position in the first place, for being good enough at her job to be trusted to run the bar, practically alone. For doing what she's told, even when she knows she shouldn't. For having to rely on cheap rent and night shifts.

She takes a deep breath and steps out from behind the bar. She scoops up Ian's pint from the couple's table and says to him quietly, 'Um, sir, I think your phone is ringing.'

She decants the beer into a takeaway coffee cup and unplugs his phone (47 per cent), placing them both on the counter in front of him. Ian has followed her, once again blocking her escape, and he's frowning at her. He's still, his eyes darting between her and the coffee cup with immense focus. The black bag is on the floor by his feet.

'Look . . . I'm really sorry. I . . . think you should go home to your boys. You've had a bit too much to drink. Take that for the road.'

Ian's gaze locks on to hers, and a slow smile creeps over his face. He doesn't move, and even though she's edging backwards, towards the fridges, she tries again. She's aiming for authoritative, but the words come out forced and feeble, like they've all been plunged underwater where sound is muffled and everything is gelatinous.

'You're bothering the customers, mate. It's time to go.'

When the assistant manager thinks about this moment again, it stretches out in front of her the way a decision does when hindsight sets in and becomes the middle act of a drama, a tragedy, her body spotlit on a stage. Something is going, will go, has gone, terribly wrong.

All of a sudden, Ian's body hardens and begins to expand. His muscles strain against his hoodie and then rip through the fabric. She watches his shoulders stretch towards the ceiling, arms lengthening and fists growing to the size of watermelons. There are two horrific crunches as his knees pop and break, his legs growing as thick as tree trunks. The transformation complete, he towers over the bar, enormous, his feet bursting out of his trainers. The beer has been thrown to the floor and his shadow casts everyone else into darkness. The heat emanating from his body is unbearable. Above him, floodlights illuminate the reddish shine of his skin. When she looks up into his eyes, she sees that they are small and black and have no pupils, like a shark's. No one seems to notice any of this, except for the assistant manager. In that moment, he's the biggest thing she's ever seen.

Ian examines her like he's seeing her for the first time. He takes in her face, her body, the pleading in her eyes and he's enraged at her daring. The kind of rage women know well, and men pretend doesn't exist. The assistant manager's exit is once again cut off by his huge, grotesque body; she can only watch him limply as he starts to speak.

Ian tells the assistant manager how ugly and pathetic she is. He describes how he'll cut to the core of her without a second thought. He's going to teach her a lesson, going to get rid of the cobwebs that must live between her legs. Ian tells her he could kill her with a single punch if he chose to, what a fucking bitch she is – and who does she think she is? – to tell him that he needs to leave. The words are a wasp burrowing into her ear. There's a bizarre, tender edge to this violence he describes – like he's reading a bedtime story to his children. Ian delivers all this in a steady, rising voice, and at last – at fucking last – the other customers turn to listen to his sermon, in mute fascination. The new hire gasps softly, and backs as far away from both Ian and the assistant manager as the bar will allow, a look of terror on her face. No one does a thing. Perhaps they are as afraid of him as she is. They're the audience now, and the assistant manager and Ian are up on the stage, one of them raging and the other one drowning.

The assistant manager could – if you asked her to – detail word for word the things Ian says to her in the next few minutes. There is nothing in there that she hasn't heard before. It's the *way* Ian says it that truly terrifies her, the furious conviction of a man who believes in his right to take what he wants, whenever he chooses. Who sees within her attempt to assert some control over something so minor – to do her job – a threat that needs eviscerating. He no longer shouts because he doesn't need to scare her any further; she is already maimed, and there's no room for her humanity at all at all at all. The assistant manager is pinned down, convinced that she is going to die trapped behind the dark and deeply scarred wood of a bar she despises. The play reaches its final act.

As Ian speaks, the assistant manager is pulling her phone from her pocket and dialling 999. She's centre-stage and her limbs have betrayed her. She trembles so much that she cannot vault over the high walls of the bar – breaking all the glass in the process, of course – the way she had always convinced herself she could, when the time came.

She wants to say, 'I think I'm going to die,' down the phone to the operator, but they won't believe her, even though there is, in the tremors of her body, a plea to survive.

'You have to send someone right now, there's an aggressive man in my bar and he's about to attack me,' the assistant manager says down the phone, her voice gluey. At her words, Ian smiles and takes a step forward with one of his huge, unwieldy legs, so he's now not just blocking her exit, but part of him is *behind* the bar itself. The new girl, now melted into the wall, lets out a tiny squeak of horror. The assistant manager gives up every part of herself and screams down the phone, 'PLEASE COME NOW!'

And things could have happened between the plea for help and its arrival, but she has no memory of it. If you were to ask her about it, all she would tell you is that she saw Ian's dead eyes and wondered why everyone sat there and did nothing as he tore her apart.

By the time the police arrive, her entire world has shrunk down to the space between them. She watches Ian's rage refocus as they approach, watches him gesticulate and shout, even as he deflates into a regular-sized man. She sees how small he becomes as he is forcibly dragged from the pub and arrested outside. She waits for someone to ask her if she's all right.

Without Ian's presence, the rest of the customers have focused inward again, their faces turned away from her own as they urgently debrief, discuss, decompress. Kay follows the police outside, a cigarette between two fingers. Ah, but she's left her lighter abandoned on the bar, so barely a minute later she's scrambling back inside, her face animated and shining with excitement. Her own misery is forgotten.

'You wouldn't believe what the police just found!' She reaches out for the assistant manager, who hasn't moved for the grief of it all, and waits for her response. When the assistant manager says nothing, Kay continues, almost gleefully, 'They searched his bag and they pulled out a huge knife! A goddamn knife! Thank goodness you weren't harmed. Oh, honey, you must be so scared. Are you okay? And do you think you could make me another double – I want to get back out there!'

A few moments later, the assistant manager locks the door of the staff toilet with shaking hands and pushes herself tight into the corner of the tiled wall. Her teeth are chattering. Her heart is slamming repeatedly against her throat. She pictures the blade slowly sliding into her belly. She thinks he would have gone for her belly – as she raised her arms to try and protect her heart, her face, surely. Perhaps he would have just gutted her and then rained blows on her as she sank, her heart broken and her blood everywhere it shouldn't be. Perhaps he would have pulled back slightly as the knife punctured her skin, so it would stick comically out of her, trapped in some state of oblivion between death and life. She could imagine that happening if he'd gone for her chest, the blow sticky and interrupted by bone.

The assistant manager realises her face is flooding with hot, fat tears, as if a dam has burst behind her eyes. She is gasping for air and control so she slaps herself across the face, slams her back against the cold, chipped tiles, digs her nails into her palms. The pain shocks her out of the panic attack and she resurfaces. She's fine. Fine fine fine.

Someone is calling her name. Kay is calling her name. The assistant manager looks at her face in the mirror and wishes she could roll her heart into a ball, like a crumpled napkin, and force it back down her throat, where it belongs. She splashes her face with water and closes her eyes.

In another universe a young woman bleeds out on to dark and deeply scarred wood, her heart now broken, her blood now everywhere it shouldn't be.

The assistant manager unlocks the bathroom door, her face completely and utterly empty, and returns to her night shift.

I wrote a poem about you, baby. It's called 'When I Put My Face Between Your Thighs, I See God'.

Weaponised Incompetence

Lia wears her vulnerability, her newness, like a cape – such unfiltered glamour! Her heart is open open open. They meet the way most young students do. Chipped glasses, crowded kitchen, steam creeping up the windows. You can split the room between those who feel at ease and those who feel clunky – like they shouldn't be here with all these silky, slippery people. But she's there anyway, the key to her dorm room on a string around her neck. Her hair curls around her shoulders like smoke. And Theo smells good. She brings yearning in her plastic wine cup, soaking it into her tongue with every sip.

Lia's smart. She's the kind of girl who always did what she was told, until suddenly she didn't, and now she's just a little too eager to let the world know. She impresses Theo with her ability in a debate. She won't let anything go – and at the start, when it's a novelty, it turns him on. She wins, and this turns him on too. Unusual, for someone as competitive as him.

The young men who think they know everything – which includes Theo – reorganise the room in intrusive ways. For example: The Taken/The Untaken. The Broken/The Unbroken. The Property/The Free for All. She is still untaken, unowned, unspoilt. None of the others hold a candle to her, Theo comments. Some disagree, some mock him for the honesty, some are swallowed up in their own thoughts. Some just aren't paying attention.

When their bodies first meet it doesn't really work. Lia doesn't like it; Theo's embarrassed. He's impatient. Or perhaps he's sympathetic? He doesn't say, and she feels shame in the lower abdomen like a vicious cramp. He takes her into his chest and holds her close, tenderly. She says nothing, does not move against him for fear he'll be repulsed by the way she seeks pleasure. She wonders if she's somehow wrong, and she stuffs anxiety down her throat like cotton wool. She says, *Let's try again when I've had some wine*, and when they try again, he brings the wine. The door is locked.

She's in love, and love has a way of shaving off the edges until everything feels smooth. Even when it isn't. Soon, it's time to move out of student dorms and into cramped houses with expensive, inefficient heating.

Lia falls over herself to prove her worth. She was taught to love men via scooping, folding, cleaning, organising, tidying, finding. She proudly packs his bags ~~with him~~ for him, helps him move. Every need, every wish, *I'm yours, I'm yours*. Theo sits on the bed, on his sheets she laundered and fitted for him, and he watches her; she glows with the thrill of it all. How radiant! How useful! How lucky he is to have a girl who loves him so earnestly, she temporarily forgets he's a grown man.

Lia ~~teaches him how to iron his shirts~~ irons his shirts for him: crisp, starched, sexy! The ironing board once

188

used to stack empty bottles of gin is now dusted off
and propped up in the little kitchen. She shows him
how to get the creases out of the sleeves, just like her
mother does, but he always forgets exactly *how* she does
it, so sweetly naive. He can't quite grasp the iron in his
clumsy, unworked hands – the steam! So hot! It hurts!
Theo doesn't like her friends – they're too loud and talk
too much – so they go to the parties he wants to attend,
and when he leaves her side to talk to his boys, she flails
in a state of abandon. She wishes he'd hold her hand.
He wishes she'd get a grip. He can't be soft and warm to
her when other people are around, and it confuses her.
Theo was taught how *not* to love someone, but he hasn't
quite come to terms with it yet.

Sometimes, when he's inside her, Lia feels a stirring
under the skin, like a train rumbling in the far distance.
Still, he has not given her an orgasm. They talk about
it and come to the conclusion that it's too hard, it's her
fault. Her body is unyielding and clenched shut like a
wired jaw. Lia has forgotten she no longer does what
she's told, and starts to fake it, to get the sex over with.
But he makes her laugh, and when he's drunk, he tells
her he loves her, and it matters, it matters.

She earns less than he does because she wants to
Make A Difference, so when it's time for them to live
together they agree that she will pay a little less rent. It's
Theo who finds the basement flat with lots of plants for
her to water and re-pot and mourn when they die from
lack of light. This arrangement, this money business,
gnaws at them. Quietly. Just a light clogging of the

throat. The grease piles up and refuses to be wiped away. They learn new things about each other that neither of them particularly enjoys – they didn't anticipate that. They learn Lia notices the mess, and therefore hates the mess, and Theo doesn't notice the mess, and is therefore unbothered. Theo likes the shelves empty and Lia likes to collect things to fill them. Lia starts and ends her days with bowls of fresh fruit and Theo insists all fruit makes his throat itch. Yes, all fruit. She ~~keeps asking him to help around the house~~ gets him to clean the kitchen one Sunday, and she's feverish with possibility. At last! The glassy relief of it!

Ah – but then – *remember the time I cleaned* – he'll be wounded, or tired, or busy, or the football's on, and besides: too many products/steps to remember/cloths/sponges and *it's all too complicated.* Theo is a hard worker with a demanding job, and he refuses to make space in his brain for things that he doesn't really care about. It's just easier if she does it. Lia starts to feel claws digging, a crater forming somewhere beneath the soles of her feet. Tension has a tendency to burrow – into the carpet, the bedding, the heart. *Love is sacrifice,* she murmurs, like she's praying, and distracts herself by thinking about how much she aches for release, for touch, for tenderness. But who will love a girl who can't bring herself to leave a man who doesn't know how to love her? Her heart, it's closing closing closing.

He smells so good. She fits so well into the curve of his body. At night, Lia reaches for him and wants to scream at herself. There's a moment when she remembers she was meant to be a girl who never did as she was told. But Lia is scared to flesh this thought out any further and falls asleep instead. In a way, she remains asleep and automated for a surprisingly long time, tricking herself into thinking she's happy.

A handful of years later, she ~~wants to rip his eyes out~~ gets Theo a cooking course for his birthday (*you always say you want to learn!*) and he is underwhelmed. She leans into his disappointment urgently, like pressing a bruise, like squeezing a peach . . . He says he'll go but then comes the rush of life – mortgage! Babies? MOT! Proposal? Holidays! Theo forgets to book it, pretends it's all so sad, so sad. Privately, he thinks his girlfriend isn't as kind as she used to be. A few years ago, she would have given him something he actually wanted.

Occasionally Theo pulls a shirt from the wardrobe and it is singed. How strange, she says. How strange. The flat creaks and groans uneasily. She comes back from a work trip and the last plant is dead. The expensive one. The gift from a cherished friend. Atop the little table by the door: her handwritten note, reminding him to water it. Theo didn't see it, not his fault, should have texted him, should have made it clearer. She looks into mirrors and sees not herself, but a woman untethered. And what was once a glow is now a forest fire: destruction, commence!

It's Sunday. Lia ~~says I'm leaving you~~ cooks a roast gently, lovingly, homemade gravy slathered on the chipped dinner plate. The heat clouds the windows, makes her sweat. The dishes pile pile pile in the sink, and she slowly eats it – a whole chicken! – until her belly strains against her jeans. Jars of seasoning that once seemed so important keep her company – sage! Onion salt! Bay leaf! The aftertaste is a little metallic, but still she does not, cannot, stop.

She ~~remembers, no, fantasises about, no,~~ *considers* a basement flat, burning. Smoke like the dark curl of hair. So many dead plants. And . . . perhaps? One body pulled out, jellied and thick. Held together only by rope. The chicken meat juices Lia's chin, and she is gleaming.

How radiant! How useful! How lucky he was to have had a girl who loved him so earnestly, she temporarily forgot he was a grown man.

A Bomb Going Off
That No One Can See

Pieter was a vigilant man by nature. Especially around women. He disliked the way they gathered and whispered amongst themselves, laughing over things they wouldn't explain. As the Head of Tourism for Mundchin, he took the reputation of his municipality seriously. Bayern, the village he and his family lived in, was becoming more popular every year, and everyone knew it was down to him. That's why, even when he rolled his eyes at the Head of Tourism's despotic insistence on intervening in all village matters, the butcher would set aside the choicest blood sausage and pork belly cuts for Hanna at the market, and the honey-seller always gave them a little extra in the pot.

And rightly so, he felt. Through Pieter's devotion, Bayern bloomed all year long. His home was picturesque and dignified, built at the foot of a giant cliff that overlooked their sunlit valley. As he took great pride in reminding everyone, Pieter's ancestors had chipped away at the granite until they'd constructed a chapel embedded in the rock, followed by a cascade of houses, until an entire village stood there. A trade route was quickly established thanks to the river just a kilometre away.

It had been his idea to build a pathway from the chapel all the way up to the cliff's precipice, suggesting it could snake through the woods and provide a popular walking route for tourists frequenting Bayern. But no one could see his genius, not even Leonora, the mayor, until he'd taken over Mundchin's tourism role and lobbied for the funds to make it happen, all by himself. Pieter had built the website, photographed the local attractions, planned out the route and secured the necessary permits. And now, the walk was Bayern's primary attraction. Hiking enthusiasts came from across the continent – although there had been a few incidents with tourists getting lost in the dense woods and never finding their way out again, which, Pieter felt, was precisely why the pathway was so important. He walked it often with Lundo, his faithful bloodhound, occasionally straying to pick wild berries for Hanna and the girls.

It was on one of these occasions, in early February, that he spotted her. It was four or so in the afternoon, and a beautiful one at that. The sky was soapy with clouds and the wind was only just starting up. Soon, the light would begin to fade. Pieter had just returned to the path with his pockets full of stoneberries and beech nuts, and the evening chill had hit him rather suddenly. And then he saw the old woman. He didn't recognise her, with her greying skin and unnaturally dark hair. The woman had spread out a dirty-looking blanket and laid her wares on the path. This wasn't the proper place or way to do things, and it irritated Pieter immediately. He was certain she didn't have a licence.

As he approached her, Lundo began creeping so closely behind his master that he threatened to trip him up. The woman was unperturbed. She must have been in her seventies or early eighties, the skin on her face sagging as she squatted over a low stool, bent over a gleam of silver that she was twisting on to a chain with a pair of pliers. Pieter cleared his throat, and she squinted up at him.

'Were you interested in buying something?'

Pieter opened his mouth, and then shut it again and swallowed. He'd spotted two trussed-up dead rabbits next to her, both missing their left hind feet. The sight alarmed him.

'I-I'm the Head of Tourism for Mundchin,' he said finally, pushing the words out with difficulty. He rubbed a hand on the back of his shorn, reddish-brown hair, and tried to regain his composure. He was being ridiculous.

'I'm responsible for tourism in the entire municipality,' he said again, expecting a change in her demeanour, but the woman simply jerked her head towards her blanket and said, 'Tourists are my best customers.'

Once again, Pieter cleared his throat. Lundo let out a low whine. 'Do you have the right licence to be selling . . . all of this?' he asked stiffly.

'Not sure why I'd need permission to sell my own work.' She heaved herself up from the stool and set the necklace down amongst the others. He noted with distaste the black rags she wore – including around her feet, bound together with rope – and wondered if she was perhaps loose in the head.

'So you don't have a licence? I would be happy to help you obtain one. With the proper paperwork, which I can take care of, and the licence fee, you could be back here in a few weeks – the correct way.'

With claw-like hands, the crone gripped a silver flask that hung around her neck and took a long, slow swig. 'I don't think so.'

Although this woman was getting on his nerves, Pieter decided to persevere with the amicable approach. He was a man of reason, after all, and had overcome his earlier nerves.

'I understand your hesitation, gentlewoman, I really do. The licence is to protect the people who live in Bayern, I'm sure you can understand. Most of us come from humble backgrounds, and we have had trouble in the past with rogue sellers.'

He bent over to inspect the rows of necklaces, earrings, bracelets, brooches – even a few belts – she was selling, feigning interest.

'These are quite something.' He hated them, of course. Pieter had never seen anything like them before, and he was repulsed, despite the obvious craftsmanship. The silver figurines were delicate, the size of a child's finger. They had been cast in such detail they were mesmerising to look at, but grotesque too. All their faces were contorted into angry or horrified expressions. Some were clutching at various body parts – their head, stomach, or heart – and others covered their faces. They seemed remarkably human, and it made him uneasy. Why on earth would anyone want to buy figures of people looking so tortured? He wanted both to lean closer and tear his eyes away – there was something about the way the fading light caught them . . . the flicker of the setting sun that made them look quite alive . . .

Instinctively, he reached out to touch a necklace. As he drew close, a horrific wail punctured the air, so agonised that it drilled right into his ear. He flinched like he'd been electrocuted.

'What was that?' Pieter snatched his hand away and took several steps backwards, looking around him wildly. 'That man! Did you hear him?'

'I heard nothing.'

'What are you talking about! You must have heard him?'

The woman was watching him in amusement. 'The wind does odd things this time of the year.' She gestured to the choker he'd been reaching for, which boasted eight of the little creatures swinging like pendants, each straining towards another, as though trying to flee hand-in-hand. 'That one's got eight souls trapped inside.'

As Pieter gaped at her, Lundo pushed at his heels anxiously, clearly desperate to leave. He had no idea how to respond to such an odd remark, and he half-feared the wail would start up again. Perhaps the man would call for help. He'd have to run back to the village. 'What's your name?'

She grinned again, revealing a missing front tooth.

Its black hole only served to unnerve him further. 'Shall we play a little game?'

'What? I asked you—'

'I heard you. I'll give my name after you pass my test.' The woman stooped to move the rabbits out of the way.

'A test? I don't need to pass your test! Have I not made it clear—' Pieter's voice caught in his throat as she straightened up to face him.

The woman had no eyes.

Two gaping holes stared at him, so black and cavernous he felt he was being sucked into them. Her nose was gone, the cartilage nibbled away to reveal grey cheekbone flecked with pink. His mouth flooded with saliva, the way it did when he was about to vomit, and he suddenly found himself unable to move or speak. He was looking directly into a dead woman's skull. Pieter blinked, and the holes were replaced with watery, grey irises. He blinked again, and she grinned. A perfectly ordinary woman. And yet.

'The game hasn't quite started,' she said.

At that point, Lundo lost whatever composure he had and began to bark furiously, backing away from them both. A shiver went through Pieter as goosebumps pricked his arms. He felt an overpowering urge to escape this strange woman as quickly as possible.

'I don't have time for this,' he stammered. 'I'm expected at the village. I have a meeting. But-but you can't be here without a permit and . . . our village . . . takes these things seriously.'

She raised an eyebrow at him, and Lundo's barks became more frantic.

'In fact,' he added weakly, 'my neighbours would have brought it to my attention if I hadn't addressed this issue first, so if I see you again tomorrow, I'll have you arrested.'

As he turned to walk away from her, she started to laugh at him. Normally he would have turned back; he had never minded confrontation when it was necessary. But that skull-face of hers stopped him, even though Pieter knew he'd just imagined it. He could feel her eyes burrowing into his own skull like a parasite as he hurried after Lundo.

Pieter barely responded to the friendly nods of his neighbours. He strode grimly through the bustle of the village market as it packed up, feeling shame creep up the back of his neck like sunburn. Away from the isolation of the woods, the hag seemed utterly harmless; an old woman playing tricks on him in a particularly eerie part of the forest. By the time he arrived at the ancestral home – one of the grandest in Bayern – that he shared with his wife and their two daughters, he was furious.

'What's wrong with Lundo?' Hanna asked as he slammed the door shut. The hound had run under the kitchen table and was cowering there, trembling. She knelt down next to him, tucking loose strands of blonde hair under her kerchief and hoisting him on to her wool trousers to scratch behind his ears. It had been Hanna who raised Lundo as a puppy, feeding him goats' milk and fashioning an apron to carry him around as he slept. She hated to see him agitated.

Pieter leant against the doorframe and tried to swallow his anger. 'He's just cold. There was a wind.'

He didn't speak much that evening, turning the encounter over in his mind like a lost game of dice. He replayed her laugh at his retreating back and cursed himself for being so pathetic. By dinner he had convinced himself that her eeriness had been entirely in his own head. He'd have to go back tomorrow and ensure she was following the law. Let her know she wasn't special.

Pieter had always felt comfortable within the calm of regulation and order. Whereas others might find conforming to meticulous details and procedures akin to wearing an invisible straitjacket, for him they acted as instructions for living as problem-free a life as possible. It was why he was so good at his job; why the residents of Bayern enjoyed living in a prosperous, immaculately kept village where crime rates were low and most people didn't bother to lock their doors at night. If anyone had asked him that evening *why* he felt so compelled to return to the woods, he would have lectured them on the profound selfishness of refusing to follow rules made for the greater good. But the truth, like always, was simpler. He could not stomach how quickly that old woman had dismissed him – scared him, even. This rage would make him foolish.

At the dinner table, Pieter kissed his wife's cheek as he sat down opposite his eldest daughter, Ada. Laura drifted in with Mish, her diminutive black cat, draped around her neck. As she joined them, her sister gave a sigh. Ada was almost sixteen, an age where she seemed irritated by everything Pieter said, especially when he tried to joke with her. But little Laura was only eight, still obsessed with him and eager for his attention. They got on handsomely. As Hanna served him a piece of rabbit slow-cooked in juniper, garlic and rosemary, his daughter shuffled around to him and pushed her head under his armpit, peering up at him excitedly.

'Did you do the walk today, Pa?'

He pressed his mouth to her hair and inhaled the sweet, cinnamony scent. 'I did, Lulu. Did you see the stoneberries on the counter?'

'I'm going to make a tart with them,' Hanna warned. 'So you can only have two, okay?'

'OKAY!' Laura shouted, slipping out from under Pieter and running into the kitchen. Ignoring the warning look from her mother, Ada stared glumly at the food. Her stomach churned as she imagined the rabbit's final moments: unable to scream, heart beating three times faster than a human, eyes rolling into the back of its head. She had seen her mother skin rabbits before, but they had always arrived dead. Hanna would lay one out on their garden table and take a cleaver, expertly cutting off the rabbit's feet at the joint to be carefully discarded. The pelt, too, would be sold. Her mother would use a sharp knife to make an incision in one of the legs, all the way up the stomach, then slowly peel the skin away from the flesh, centimetre by centimetre, with a soft sucking sound. The strain of the peel would often cause the rabbit's gut to burst open. Unfazed, Hanna would tenderly remove the intestines, taking care not to rupture them. She would then typically rub them in a paste of salt and rosemary and leave them in the sun for several days to dry out. Afterwards, they'd be sliced into thin strips and fried with onions and bulbs of black garlic. One of Pieter's favourites. As a child, Ada had always wondered why the rabbits did not bleed when they were torn apart like that.

'One day I'll be a vegetarian,' she mumbled into the plate.

'Maybe, but today is not that day,' her mother said, in a tone that discouraged further complaints. Ada looked down at the flesh in front of her, the gamey smell of it, and wondered if she would vomit.

'I'm not sure I can eat this.'

'Oh, but you *will* eat it,' Hanna said sharply. 'That rabbit cost us a small fortune. The men who hunted it were out in the forest for several days to find the meat we all need to survive. And I spent hours preparing this for you. You're lucky that you live in a house that can provide for you so well.'

Ada turned desperately to Pieter. 'Father?'

'Your mother's right, Ada. I'm sorry, but the rule in our home is that we are grateful for the food we have.' Pieter, who still yearned for the days when his eldest had seen him as a hero, tried to catch Ada's eye and smile at her. But her head was lowered as she speared a potato with her fork, and she didn't look up again for a long time. Not even when her father snuck a chunk of rabbit off her plate with a wink when her mother wasn't watching.

After dinner Pieter sat by the fireplace with Laura nestled in one arm, and cleaned his pipe in preparation to pack it. Ada had vanished with a book, and Hanna had turned to the dishes with her mouth set in a hard line. She had long given up on asking her husband to contribute to keeping the house clean and well-organised – even though the demand for this level of tidiness only ever came from him. It did, however, remain a source of tension between them, simmering away in the undercurrent of their marriage. The older Hanna became, the more disillusioned she felt by the life stretching out in front of her.

Still, she let the cat climb into the large pocket of her apron, and as he snoozed she made the tart lovingly, spreading cream that she'd whipped herself on to the top and smoothing the edges, dusting the whole thing off with icing sugar and adding a sprig of mint to the centre. It sat, untouched, on the oak dining-room table – the biggest in the village. Pieter had hired a carpenter to work on it directly outside their home, so passers-by could see how grand it would become. She watched him brush his hand over it, checking for dust, as he carried their sleeping daughter up to bed and tenderly tucked her in. Hanna had just settled into the warm patch he left behind when her husband returned and nudged his way in beside her.

'That damn cat,' he growled when he saw Mish

cradled in her lap. 'We spoilt her with it and now it leaves hair everywhere.'

'Well, *I* clean this house every day,' Hanna said pointedly, 'and it doesn't bother me.'

They said nothing for a few moments, Pieter watching her stroke the cat as if daring him to move it. Eventually he spoke.

'Without you this home, this family, would fall apart.'

Hanna relaxed against him. 'It would.'

'Without you, I am nothing.'

'You aren't.'

'The day I die will be the day your greatest burden lifts.'

'Stop that!' she laughed, nudging his rounding belly. 'Don't even joke about it.'

'It's true! I'm the useless one of the family.' Pieter gently stroked the soft pad of Mish's paw. The sleeping cat twitched.

'Now you're being stupid. In fact, do you know what I was thinking about, earlier?'

'What?'

'Jasker, when the tree caught his leg.'

Pieter sighed heavily. 'That was a terrible day.'

'It was horrible.' Hanna's eyes were fixed on the flames dancing in the grate of their marbled fireplace. Pieter had insisted on importing the marble, even though it was ridiculously opulent for their house filled with wood. But at least it was easy to clean.

'I thought of him because I saw Marilene at the market, and I almost never see her here these days. She usually shops all the way over the mountain, closer to her town.'

'Mmm.'

'But that day, when the tree fell on his leg and crushed it, well – the whole village saw what kind of a man my husband was. You stayed by his side for hours, hacking away at the trunk with your stupid little knife. You called for help. You even paid a messenger to run all the way to Hörgen – nine kilometres away! To tell Marilene the news. How long was it that you stayed with him?'

'Until he was free.'

'But how many hours?'

'Seven. Maybe eight.'

'Yes. And when I arrived there with food and tea for everyone, I found you by his side, promising him that he was going to be all right. You kept him alive. You paid the expenses when he had to go all the way to the capital to amputate.' Hanna tore her eyes away from the flames and stared at him fiercely. 'You're a good man. We need you around this house.'

'Of course you do.' Pieter scooped Mish out of Hanna's lap, startling him awake. 'Without me, this place would be covered in cat hair, for god's sake.' He stood up with the cat held firmly in his hands and roughly deposited it beside Lundo. 'It'll ruin our sofa if you let it sleep up there.'

Only Laura and Mish slept well that night. Ada dreamt a rabbit was sitting at the end of her bed, missing its left hind leg. It begged her for help in a tiny, high-pitched voice, even when she tearfully informed it that there was nothing she could do. Pieter slept fitfully, and his constant movement kept Hanna half-awake and irate until the early hours. By five, he was itching to get back on to his beloved path. He had planned out the speech he would give the woman in the woods and rose earlier than the rest of his family, kissing Hanna on her warm forehead as he slipped out of the room.

As the sky began to lighten, he threw a few logs into the kitchen stove and lit the kindling. He made sure to measure out enough water for Hanna and Ada too, knowing they would appreciate it when they shuffled down the stairs with their identical, sleepy faces.

The coffee was strong, the way he liked it, but once he'd poured out his own cup he added a little milk and sugar for his girls and left the pot close enough to the flame to stay warm. Far too much time was spent trying to tempt Lundo from under the table with a morsel of rabbit. But the dog refused to budge, growling at Pieter when he got on his hands and knees and attempted to drag him out.

It was bitingly cold when he left the family home alone, armed with a copy of the bylaws and trade regulations of Mundchin, his name emblazoned on the front in red. No one saw him enter the forest. He would have been wearing a brown overcoat and a grey jumper made of sheep's wool – colours that wouldn't stand out on a February morning. No one realised until much later that Mish had followed him, his little black body trotting behind Pieter, stark against the snow.

At first, Hanna was unconcerned, although a little

annoyed, when Pieter did not return for the lunch she had prepared. She had bought freshly caught mirror carp at the Sunday market and grilled it across hot coals in their garden. She drizzled it with lemon and a sprinkling of dill and white pepper and served it with a salad of tomatoes, cabbage and bread made by their neighbour. She assumed Pieter had been invited to eat at someone's home, which happened often.

But by the early evening, she was angry. Lundo had been unusually irritating, tailing her so closely it caused her to trip up several times. She instructed the girls to take him out and wash him with a hose as she cut the first slice of stoneberry tart and ate it alone, glancing at the front door whenever she heard a noise. They had roast chicken with boiled potatoes and fried courgette with double cream for dinner, and Hanna snapped, 'I don't know!' when Laura asked her where Pa was.

When her youngest was safely asleep, Hanna sank two glasses of wine and rehearsed the argument she'd have with him in her head. If her eldest was bothered by her father's absence, she didn't show it. It was only when Hanna woke at the 7 a.m. light with a dry mouth and a throbbing head and found that her husband was not in the bed next to her, nor asleep on the sofa downstairs, nor in either of the girls' bedrooms, that she felt the first pangs of fear.

In the months that followed his disappearance, many of the villagers would search the surrounding woods for Pieter. They would organise shifts of four or five people and head out armed with hot flasks of sweet tea and strips of jerky. Mish's frozen little body was found a week into the search, half-eaten and mutilated. Hanna kept this information from Laura – though not from Ada – and buried the body behind the house, where she usually gutted the chickens. Hanna herself would go out alone for long stretches, returning tear-streaked and exhausted. She only stopped when Ada told her Laura was terrified that she too would not come back. The family settled into a rhythm of constantly waiting for him to walk through the door, glancing up whenever they heard footsteps. Lundo took to following Hanna around closely, insistent on sleeping on Pieter's side of the bed. Laura lost her playful edge, crying at things she hadn't previously noticed, like the hairless body of a baby bird that fell out of its nest in their garden. She asked for Mish endlessly. Ada and Laura started creeping into each other's beds, waking up sweat-soaked and tangled, as if they'd fought each other in their sleep.

When June came, the weather finally turned and the sun crept out, throwing Bayern into warm light. Sunflowers bloomed and a gentle wind blew across the wheat fields, making it seem like the earth itself was waving up at the sky. Ada started to walk the pathway again. On the verge of seventeen, she had spent the last few months in the library, secretly preparing to leave for a city – any city – hoping to further her studies. Hoping her mother would be able to cope with her absence, too. It was on one of these sun-filled walks that she stumbled across an old woman selling beautiful silver figurines on the edge of the forest.

Ada gasped as she approached them, captivated. The jewellery seemed to pulsate with life. She had never encountered such artistry before, and was eager, asking questions and complimenting several of the pieces. The woman watched intently, her eyes scanning the girl's face. She nodded approvingly when Ada asked if she was allowed to pick up an adorned belt, each figure dangling from a chain, all positioned side by side, as if they were on a merry-go-round. Or as if they had just been hanged. One of her most expensive pieces.

'There's forty souls in that belt.'

'That's . . . I . . . I've never seen anything like this before!' Ada exclaimed, choosing to politely ignore the odd comment. She wondered if the woman had spent a long time by herself as she wrapped the dark leather around her waist. The figures jangled slightly, clinking cheerfully against each other as she turned one way and then the other.

'It's incredible.' She marvelled at how the little men and women's expressions seemed to change as they caught the light. She'd stand out in the big cities with a belt as unusual as this. It was only when Ada had emptied the entire contents of her purse into the artist's outstretched hands that she spotted a pendant that made her freeze. She crouched down and bent so close that her nose was almost touching it. The silver man was kneeling, both hands drawn up to his heart and clutching a pipe. On his face, there was a ferocious scowl, his mouth open in a silent scream. He looked like he was in the middle of a tumultuous prayer, or perhaps an argument. Although she knew it must be a trick of the light, Ada could almost swear she saw smoke rising from the pipe.

'You like that one too, I see. Let's play a little game for it,' the woman said in her ear.

Distracted by the gleam of the metal, Ada simply murmured, 'A game? What are the rules?'

'I'm going to look into your soul and see what it's made of. If I like what I see in there, I'll take it – unless you stop me from getting in, of course.'

Ada laughed out loud as she straightened up. 'I'm not sure I—'

She let out a gasp, a shiver running through her. She suddenly found herself centimetres away from an owlish, emaciated face, with gaping holes where its eyes should have been. Its mouth was open in a skeletal grin, and as she stared, a maggot crawled out of the black void and fell to the earth below. Ada felt as if many hundreds of hands were gripping the edges of her dress and dragging her towards the creature. She tried to take a step back, but those hands forced her into submission. Wind whipped between them, stinging her, and a powerful hum rose in her ears – she was tipping forward – the beak-mouth opening . . .

And then, in front of her, Ada saw it clearly. The cat – their cat, their Mish – squirming between the woman's hands and screeching loudly. She tried to move, to snatch him away from her, but her limbs felt marionetted, no longer her own.

'Mish,' she tried to say. The words stuck in her throat.

Horrified, she watched the old woman bend her beak-face and tear a chunk out of the cat, so large and deep it exposed his tiny, twitching heart. Ada was certain the cat was screaming, but the wind was so strong she couldn't hear anything beyond it. Her arms hung uselessly by her side. As the bird-creature ate, she felt herself pulled in closer and closer to its bloodied, dripping maw—

'*Ada! Ada! Ada!*' Her father's voice was explosive and urgent, startling her out of the trance. It was as though a bucket of icy water had been dumped over her. Her limbs seemed to reawaken, and the terrifying pulling sensation vanished. Ada realised she was kneeling, her head bowed down. She placed her hands on the ground and pushed her fingers into the cold dirt, searching for something to hold on to. Her cheeks were hot and tear-stained. Slowly, the forest came back to her.

'Are you all right, sweetheart?' the old woman asked, squinting down at her in concern. When Ada finally worked up the courage to raise her head, she saw only a wrinkled human face staring back. No blood, no beak, no cat. The woman stretched out a hand, and after a moment of hesitation, Ada took it.

'I'm sorry. I don't know what happened, I must have fainted, I must have a – a fever. Haven't been sleeping much,' she mumbled, wiping her face. She took several shuddering breaths, and then glanced quickly at the pendant. Her father's voice still rang in her ear, and more than ever before, she wished she could turn around, run home and fling herself into his arms.

'That necklace. It looks just like . . .' She swallowed and shook her head. 'Sorry. It just reminds me of someone.'

'People often say that. You won this round of my game, by the way. Few do.'

'I see.' Truthfully, Ada couldn't even remember what she was talking about. Her forehead throbbed furiously and she badly needed to lie down. She felt like she'd been hit over the head with a stack of books. The image of her cat's twitching body looped over and over in her mind.

The woman finished wrapping the belt in scraps of fabric and scratched her chin, considering. Eventually, she told the girl, 'My name is Seelendieb.' She held out the parcel.

'It's a very, um . . . different name.' Ada forced a weak smile on to her face. 'Powerful. I guess you aren't from around here, with a name as rare as that.' But 'rare' wasn't quite the right word. Ada had studied German for several years and was a little startled that anyone would have been given a name as ominous as that. Soulthief. She wondered if she'd fallen asleep back at the library, and this bizarre dream was her punishment.

The woman threw her head back and laughed loudly, her grey hair shaking. 'If you say so. Yours means noble, does it not?'

'Um, yes. That's what my father told me.'

'Here.' Seelendieb scooped up the pendant that looked so much like Pieter and fastened the silver chain around Ada's neck.

'It's yours. No one else was going to buy this one anyway. The material is too unforgiving.' The necklace felt uncomfortably warm to the touch, and Ada wondered again if she was coming down with sickness. When she tried to thank Seelendieb, the old woman simply shook her head.

'One day we'll meet again, and I might not be so generous.'

It was only when Ada was halfway home, her hand pressed over the little man around her neck, that she realised she'd never told the woman her name. She stopped in her tracks, and half-turned, even though nothing in the world would have made her go back.

What Ada did not see was the enormous, gaunt bird, flecked with grey. It followed her with wings that did not make a sound, its head turning as she did. Had it been low enough for the human eye to perceive, she'd have realised the bird's entire skull was exposed to the elements, two yawning holes where its eyes should have been.

Palate Cleanser III

The quickest way to make a person want something is to tell them that they cannot have it. The all-girls' school was twinned with an all-boys' school, which meant they would do their summer concerts and services and annual plays together. Every term, at church, they put up metal barriers between the girls' and the boys' seating area. Literal metal barriers, the kind used to cordon off building sites, except there was no tarp to keep out prying eyes. The girls would whisper and laugh and drink the boys in with glee. I couldn't tell you what the boys thought – they pretended they weren't bothered – but I'm sure it was disconcerting. The atmosphere in the church was always so charged up and *exciting*. The girls prepared for it. There were the absurdly long polyester skirts hastily rolled up above their knees, leaving a faint doughnut-shaped ring around their waists. Cheap, chalky foundation, eyeliner, flavoured lip gloss that everyone put on and immediately licked off. Little earrings shaped like bows. Top two – top three, for the bolder ones! – shirt buttons undone.

Life at an all-girls' school is an extremely sexy time for a fourteen-year-old girl who doesn't know a single boy, at an age when boys are the social currency. She's nearly fifteen. She knows she's not got long left.

I don't know any girls like that, though, thankfully! All the girls I know are roundly fierce and effervescent, all the girls I know choose self-adoration and, when they're ready for it, pleasure. All the girls I know have this thing they do where they read your mood just by how you greet them. And when they want to, they have a way of making everyone feel so special and so wonderful and so pretty. And it's so heartfelt, you can watch them do it all night long and still light up when they turn around and do it to you. All the girls I know and love kiss girls and press their faces into each other's necks, drink in their smells and tastes and fall asleep holding hands.

Menace

The first time it happens, no one realises what they're witnessing. Not even later, when the vanishings dominate the headlines, do the people in the park realise they were there, front row, when it began.

It takes place outside, on the kind of summer afternoon where the heat is so extreme that bored children are cracking eggs open on sizzling car bonnets, marvelling at the hardening glisten of the yolk. In a park at the edge of the city, the mothers sit under the shade of leafy trees, hushing others around them or pressing their noses into the tiny, wriggling toes of their babies and inhaling the sweet, damp smell. There are squeezy tubes of fruit yogurt and bland snacks for the babies, and iced coffees for the mothers. The grass has lost all its moisture, becoming dusty and hard.

One of the mothers sits with her toddler and indulges his latest obsession, a book about dinosaurs. He smashes his pudgy fist into a drawing of a diplodocus and squeals when the mother growls into his neck. He'd been terrified of dinosaurs until she told him about the asteroid hitting the earth, how all the soot had blocked out the sun and barely anything had survived. Then he had been terrified of asteroids, until she lied and told him the sun had swallowed them all. And even though she's the closest one to the situation, when it happens – which is imminently – she doesn't notice it either. Which is a shame.

There is a muffled sort of bang, like the thud of a large sack of flour falling off a countertop. The mother is startled; she and her child jump in unison. A few other heads pop up in mild surprise, turning towards its source: a copse of trees that surround a shallow lagoon, often avoided for its stench. The little boy begins to cry, and the mother bounces him in her arms, holding him close to her and murmuring, *What a brave, brave boy you are.* She one-handedly piles their snacks and books and toys and sun hats and water bottles and sunscreen and changing bag into the stroller then awkwardly drags it across the grass until she's much further away from the lagoon. By the time her son calms down, they have both moved on from the strange noise.

Nothing else really happens after that, and the distant jingle of an ice-cream van breaks the sudden, communal stillness. Other mothers curl back into their babies with soft coos, a group of youngsters spread themselves back out on to the grass with loud laughs. The heat is demanding, and who has the energy to go poking about in mosquito-ridden waters, anyway? Not in this weather.

And so, no one reacts and no one notices a thick cloud of what appears to be smoke rising from the copse, undulating like a black wave rising directly from the earth. They do not hear the low buzz – almost a moan? – that accompanies the mass as it scatters across the sky and quickly melts into the distance. Nothing changes. Yet.

A few days later, MISSING posters populate the park, zip-tied to lamp posts and hammered into trees. Now laminated in black and white, the lined face of a woman in her sixties is sprinkled into the trees like sugar. The black-and-white image isn't the best quality; it flattens her and makes her look much older than she is, with a jowly face and a thin mouth. Underneath this image the poster reads, *Mother and wife, Joyce, missing since Wednesday. Last seen in this park – have you seen this woman? All information welcome, please call* – and then a number. Someone had handwritten it on every single poster, neat, rounded digits in red ink.

The thing about Joyce, though, is that she is neither young nor beautiful, and this works against her. She might have been the first to go missing, but she doesn't stay the only one for long. By autumn her image has melted away amongst the five other missing faces. People are spooked by all the posters and what this might mean for the safety of their park, with its luscious trees and poorly lit paths, especially now with the sun setting earlier and earlier. And the weeks pass; things do not change. You'd think a story like this would be everywhere – six women vanished, in the same part of the clean, shiny city. And you'd be right of course, but probably not the way you imagined.

When the image of the seventh woman goes up, the users of the park complain there's more black-and-white than green. *Where are the police?* they mutter amongst themselves. *Why can't we just enjoy our park in peace? Haven't we earned that small pleasure?*

And it is this spark that ends up setting the whole story on fire. One of the local residents does it. An older man – a bachelor by choice, he claims – calls up a local reporter and complains about how dreadfully slow the police are, how none of the women have been found, how the park-lovers have formed a support group to accompany each other on their daily walks. The reporter asks if anyone from the group has reached out to the families of those women, and the man is quite baffled by that question. *Why would we speak to strangers?*

The story goes viral and divides the internet. Some are disgusted by the support group's lack of concern for the missing women, which becomes a national scandal in and of itself. Others focus on the police, because really, how incompetent can a force be to find not a single shred of evidence or a lead for *seven* women? What is really going on here?

At this point, the sleuths and the armchair detectives join the dots. It's not just seven women, but hundreds, who have disappeared in the past few months, all over the country. Every day it seems there's another name in the headlines, another family camping outside their elected officials' offices with blown-up pictures. There is 24-hour news coverage and fundraisers and conspiracy theories and hashtags and T-shirts and vigils. Speculation buzzes with the grim determination of flies around manure.

Another strange thing begins to happen: every so

often, people report bizarre swarms of bees in their neighbourhoods, erratic in the sky. They move in co-ordinated curls and loops. The noise emitting from these bees is unsettling; a thrum, a wailing lament that pushes into stomachs and burrows deep into marrow.

But who knows what to do with that kind of information?

By December, the mysterious fate of the women – their numbers swelling – grips the nation. Everyone talks about the women and the bees and everyone is worried that their sister or mother or aunt or grandma or cousin or friend will be next. Or that *they* will be next. The women wonder if it is painful. Police forces from different states furiously try to understand how hundreds can simply disappear with no evidence, no pattern and no link. Some have hard lives, some really don't – some simply vanish while doing the washing-up. Even the young, beautiful, pale ones are going now, their parents pleading for information and holding up headshots for the cameras. Grief becomes so commonplace it beds amongst the flower beds and garden hedges, which the bees will nuzzle in the spring. And, well, there's something terrible about getting so used to vanishing women, but that is exactly what happens. No bodies are found. There are marches and demonstrations, but there's also an election cycle, and that's really quite important. The newly elected President promises unprecedented levels of funding to explain the unexplainable, once and for all . . . but he's talking about the bees, of course. The *bees* are the real problem by now. They have started to *hunt*.

No one knows exactly when, or why, the declining bee population starts to reverse. It doesn't make any sense. Scientists are at first ecstatic, heralding the dawn of a new, lush era for the planet. But the thing about the bees is that they are unpredictable, misbehaving and altogether terrifying. This particular species appears to be aggressive and intelligent, banding together to chase people down the street for no discernible reason. A few unlucky souls who swipe at the bees with electric fly swats or other such weapons find themselves slowly and agonisingly stung to death, the bees' spent little bodies forming mounds next to the swollen corpses they leave behind. They hover outside homes and workplaces, crawl inside ventilation shafts and cause structural damage to the public libraries, hospitals and offices, or swarm entire vehicles for hours at a time, leaving petrified, sweating drivers trapped inside their cars. The more women disappear, it seems, the more the bees rage.

It must be said, the bees are a *menace*.

We are rapidly developing solutions, the scientists say. They argue ferociously with the religious leaders, who understand *exactly* what is going on. It is at best a warning, the leaders say, and at worst, the end of us all.

Don't be stupid, the new President says. They insist he wear a bespoke beekeeping suit, every time he steps outside. *This country remains undefeated in military history. We've got the biggest, strongest economy in the world. We can handle a few rogue bees.*

But even he has to admit it's taking longer than he

would like. And there are costs. Across the country, without women, households are collapsing, care homes are disintegrating and schools are effectively being run by the pupils. Men are feeding their children so much cereal for dinner it triggers a national wheat shortage. The pornography industry crumbles, wiping a cool $12 billion from the economy. The new President declares: it's them or us. The scientists have finally figured it out, he says. There's a vague promise in a speech somewhere to reverse the decline of civilisation, which does well for his approval ratings, and then there's a taskforce, specially created, with the sole aim of eradicating the bees. And then, of course, there is fierce opposition from those who worship the bees and the reckoning they bring – who have taken to walking around in loose, flowing black, brown and yellow robes, their arms outstretched. If the bees land on them, it is a great honour. The worshippers frequently warn of the apocalyptic consequences attacking the bees would bring. So it is no surprise that when the President announces his next move, they swiftly take to the underground bunkers.

It begins a year to the day since that mother – who knows *what* became of her? – sat in that park with her little boy, reading him his dinosaur book, unwittingly a few feet away from the very epicentre of it all. She was, or is, a single mother. If something happened to her, her little boy will be in someone else's care now.

Like every good reckoning, there is humour to be found. Engineers in beekeeper suits attach comically huge nozzles to every building in the country which stands over sixty feet high. A nozzle for every square foot, yards and yards of slender tubes running along sidewalks like reams of freakish spaghetti. Imagine the cost of it all! People watch from their windows. Some of them, the ones with young kids, make signs to stick to the glass, saying things like, *Bees belong in flowers!* And *We love you, Mr President.*

The taskforce has an endless budget, but even with all that shiny, clean money, it takes them almost half a year to rig the entire country. The bees hover near the engineers as they work, curious. Often, two or three of the more daring bees will split from the group and creep closer, landing on concrete or steel or glass or Perspex and resting their wings on their backs. Perhaps they are scouts, sent to assess the situation. Some cities report attempts by the bees to chew through the spaghetti strings, as if they can sense the danger approaching. But even working together, their little jaws cannot puncture those cables, and they soon lose interest.

For weeks now, everyone has been warned that they must stay inside on this specific day. The President, who is, by now, not new and much greyer, promises them that this is it – the end of the ordeal.

And then the day comes. The army, clad in protective gear and gas masks, apprehends anyone who is brave enough to attempt breaking this rule. The country collectively holds its breath. And then, at precisely 11 a.m., 400 million cubic feet of custom-made pesticide is released into the air.

First, it is very quiet. It must not have worked. The President's suit is soaked through with sweat; the scientists frantically discuss calculations and margins of error; the engineers worry about nozzle malfunctions or distribution efficiency, until—

Screams. *Screams.* SCREAMS. Chaos rips through the air like a detonation, like a murder, like an ending. Everywhere is black and fuzzy and calcified as the bees lose their bearings and career into the windows and the sidewalks. They move as if on fire, as if swallowing acid, as if they've been reining themselves in out of compassion until now. The pain is unbelievable and the hours pass, slow and sticky. Their terror is so profound it has a smell (rotting cabbage) and a sound (a child drowning, over and over again). Citizens stuff their heads under pillows and pull blankets over themselves, and when they finally emerge, the bees are gone. The air smells like the aftermath of chemical wildfire – that is to say, like death. But there are no bodies.

The day concludes in silence, almost dreamlike. The President prepares his victory speech. He tries to forget the sound and ignore the smell. His hair, at this point, is utterly grey. Then—

Pop pop pop. The women vanish. Every last one of them. Even the President's assistant, whose name he thinks might be Mary. Quicker and hungrier and angrier, they go. And then—

Softly, as the dawning sun races upwards, great plumes of what looks like smoke drift into the air. The bees start to block out the light, a sea of ash settling like a shroud across the sky. They move as one – languid, lazy at first. But those who are watching can see them pick up speed. The President's shiny, grey face is broadcast around the world as he begins his victory speech.

What will happen when the sun cannot shine?

A low whine begins – soon it will become frenzied enough to shatter tiny, delicate earbones. How beautiful. How mesmerising. How deadly.

God, women are easily offended these days, aren't they?

Liquorice

I've got a handful of speculums in my bag. They clink together as I walk, sounding like the sharpening of a knife, making me sweat. She said they were unused, but who knows?

No one likes to talk about vaginal discharge and how it coats those duckbill-shaped speculums. Except this time, a nurse commented on mine as she did my smear and I felt like a frog being dissected. A speculum enters like an electric shock, and the muscle in my bum always spasms. Legs butterflied, I felt a little nauseated. In that stuffy room which smelt of hand sanitiser and cucumbers, the nurse kept telling me to relax – but how do you soften your body and smile as a stranger is prising you apart? I wish shame got me high, because then I'd have a great fucking time every time they shove/slide/insert/ spear spear spear. I've got a tilted uterus and can't bear to be weighed – things that make me A Handful at the clinic. I can't even put a mirror down there to look at it. Some feminist I am. Usually when I'm getting my smear test I try to distract myself by listing all the words I know for vagina (yoni, pussy, cunt, quim, scared flower, muff, lady garden, punani, twat, *down there*, gash, slit, flap, front bottom, snatch, and so on), searching for one I could say out loud without, you know, dying of embarrassment. Then I thought about how, as little girls, our parents pass down cutesy little names such as 'cookie' and 'frou frou' and 'dinky' and 'minnie' like our vulvas and vaginas are silly or shameful or hidden things. Then I end up thinking about my friend Beya, who once said worship and hatred are just splinters apart from each other. And lying there, with that speculum literally pulling my vagina open, I think I understand what she means. It makes me think of another story she told me, about chainsaws and how they were invented to use on women's bodies during childbirth. Help and harm are so often interchangeable.

I don't even like liquorice. But Beya told me it makes you taste better when someone's going down on you. I'm worried that I taste disgusting, like sour sweat maybe, or that I smell unwashed and unclean even though I *do* wash, I *am* clean. Now I should probably google how much discharge is normal, just in case I'm not. I sometimes think, with a shiver of anxious pleasure, about a warm, gentle tongue, and how I rarely let anyone do it to me, because . . . well, because the idea of someone seeing it directly, seeing *me* directly, makes me clench. Give me mediocre sex any day, over that kind of exposure.

Anyway, did you know that when it's harvested, liquorice is viscous? The roots produce a thick sweetness, an aromatic flavour. Unique. They say it is medicinal. They say it cures dysfunction. But in order to extract the mucus from the root, you need to cut, strip and pulverise the flower. They say pain gives birth to art. I'd rather it bloomed from my laughter instead.

Anyway. When the nurse was done, I slid off the bed and stood there, pigeon-toed, waiting for her to turn around so she wouldn't see me put my underwear back on. And that's when she made her comments. She said, 'I've noticed you've got an awful lot of discharge. Do you know what thrush is?' Her tone made it clear she thought that my discharge was a bad thing – or, perhaps, a thing to be concerned about. My face grew hot and I was really upset, but in the clinical rush, I couldn't seem to push the words out to defend myself and my discharge. And then she left the room, left the . . . well. I bought black liquorice at the corner shop and chewed on it as the dried gel chafed my thighs, thinking about what I could do with this bag full of metal speculums I stole as they clink-clink-clinked against my hip. I didn't even hesitate when she left the room. I just took them. I know what thrush is. I just wanted to show her I wasn't going to let her humiliate me like that. The liquorice gummed up between my teeth and made me feel sick, but I kept going.

Pandora

(EXTRACTS FROM *Stories to Tell Your Five-Year-Old*)

This idea that destruction spawns from the actions of a woman is stupid. They would have done it anyway, even if I had said no. Of course I lifted the lid from the jar, just as they expected me to.

I was created for the purpose of punishment, which is a dangerous thing. You have no idea what it means to be so powerful, you cannot physically remain seated. It's relentlessly painful, like teeth gnawing on bones, like tiny metal shards crawling up your veins. My skin even cracked open from the heat that radiated from shrivelling lungs: a body aflame and triumphant. When the waiting became unbearable, I began. I peeled away the damaged flesh and allowed the blood to pool at my feet, mixing it with earth until it became a sticky, scarlet clay. The gods and goddesses watched in silence as I worked, my lips disintegrating and my hair falling out. When the jar was finally finished, I watched as they flung it on to the ground to see if it would shatter. It didn't.

They filled it with diseases, pestilence, hatred . . . all the different flavours of death. Once they handed it back to me, I felt at ease, even as my teeth began to crumble.

I knew what they wanted me to do. Of course the darkness began oozing like a sore. What they did not, could not anticipate was the way I ripped the skin of my mouth wide open, extending my jaw beyond what was possible, pulling the flesh until it stretched far enough to encompass all the misery seeping out from that jar of blood and dirt. The gods recognised their defeat. I swallowed it all. I held it all.

I didn't do it for anyone except myself. Because I could, and because I enjoyed the idea of wielding absolute control over evil for aeons to come. And that's how it would have been, had there been any kind of gratitude from you humans. But there wasn't, and so you didn't deserve my sacrifice.

I know the stories painted me as beautiful. But I wasn't. There is no beauty in the kind of power that I possess, only fury.

I am Pandora, the coiled viper

Fuck Your Lexicon

They called it a misprint at first because no one had a better word for it. But a misprint is not the right way to talk about what happened to us when the meanings of the words in the dictionaries began to change. Slowly, methodically, and then all at once; like vines creeping up a house and choking out the light. The definitions changed in *all* dictionaries, even the ones in different languages. In *all* the bookshops. How does that even happen?

Some people started calling it an illness.

The news fixated on it, and I don't think that helped. Every day, they would hold up a dictionary to read out the changing words. They coined a term for it: 'the before times' and 'the new times'. Everyone was afraid of what the new times might bring. Often, when people are afraid, they turn on each other. We know this of course because The Horrors have persisted for . . . well, I don't know how long for. Before I was born. There was a world, once upon a time, that allowed people – all people, even people like me – to choose who was in charge. According to the stories, the people chosen were only allowed to be in charge for a handful of years at a time – how *unusual*. Sid says there were rules back then too, though, just different rules. The army wasn't allowed to do half the stuff they do now, like disappearing people. There weren't nearly as many wars, or laws. Once, Sid told me – and I'm not even sure if he was telling the truth – there wasn't even such thing as a curfew. People could just go and do whatever they wanted, any time they wanted. I said it sounded like heaven and he got real quiet and told me I was wrong. But wrong or not, it was better than what we have now. No one can tell me otherwise.

Of course I wanted a copy of the dictionary. Everyone did; it became a dangerous thing to possess. To stay safe from suspicion, I acted like I wasn't interested in any of it. I pretended to be sick of the news making us all feel like we were going to die; the way they kept reading out the new words like everything we knew was over. But really, it was because I wanted to take a little sliver of whatever was going on and possess it for myself. I wanted to sit and read the whole thing alone, undisturbed, and soak up some of the magic – or whatever it was – that was in those books. Just a little bit of it, to feel more in control.

Clearly I wasn't alone there. Whenever the shops were allowed to open, people rampaged through them looking for the things. Before they got banned they would raid the shelves and buy up every copy, fighting each other if they had to. We heard stories of people's trucks being crashed into after a haul and all the dictionaries being stolen, or fistfights taking place between desperate, hungry people. They sold them for ten, twenty times their value. Many of them were going for *thousands* a pop. I didn't know anyone with that kinda money.

People are resourceful, though. Like one of our neighbours, Sid, who got real drunk the night our neighbourhood decided we were gonna break the government curfews again and stayed out in our park, drinking hooch and raspberry lemonade. I always liked old Sid, even though lots of people on our block hated him because he was an ex-army guy, and they still saw him as the enemy. But the thing about Sid was that, even though he never shaved and you could always smell the sweat off him, like he'd just been digging in the dirt, he despised the army. If you gave him just five minutes of your time, he'd rage about them until you were trying to wriggle away.

The night we all broke curfew was a gorgeous, clear one, and someone had built a bonfire. We were nervous; people like us get shot at before we get the chance to explain, so we were all drinking more than might have been wise. Sid was off by himself as usual, under a sad, old willow tree that had had some of its pretty leaves hacked away. I left the warm, welcome glow of the fire and went over to sit next to him. It felt safer under there too, like we'd be able to get away if anything happened. I wonder now if that's why he chose it.

Sid was half-gone when I sat down, but I didn't mind too much. I was pretty buzzed myself. He was quiet at first, trying to work out exactly who it was in the dark next to him, but then he said, 'Oh, it's you, Malarkey.'

My name's not Malarkey. But Sid always calls me that

when he's drunk because he says I remind him of his buddy in the army. I could never work out if that was an insult or not. I mean, I keep my hair short because it's easier, but I'm very obviously a woman, I think.

Sid rambled on a bit about the corrupt government and the fake coup and the real war. All the usual stuff. Not many people listened to Sid when he got like this. It's not that he was a conspiracy theorist. We knew it was true, after all, that the start of the war had meant the end of all that freedom we used to be so proud of – not that I was there for any of it – and that the man in charge had thieved and tricked his way in and set The Horrors into motion. And then he found new people to blame for all our problems, so the enemy slowly grew and grew. Eventually we'll just be fighting the entire world until there's no one left to fight but each other.

After a couple of decades most people around here were either dead, grieving their dead or too beaten down to do anything other than survive. Not Sid, though. I've never met a guy more fired up – it was a miracle he'd stayed alive.

So it was that night, that Sid told me about a dream where he'd taken his van and broken into a warehouse. He'd found one hundred copies of the Merriam-Websters, and made enough to retire, buy an exit permit, and move to the Seychelles. I froze up when he told me that, because by then those books had been outlawed; anyone who found them had to 'burn or return'. The news was reporting all the army raids, and showing us videos shot from helicopters of massive piles of book burnings.

'Good thing it was just a dream, Sid,' I said carefully when he stopped talking. Sid rubbed the back of his shaved blond head and didn't say anything else.

The next day, after I got home from work, I knocked on his door and asked him in a whisper if he had any copies left. Sid looked at me for a long time, his face mostly in shadow, and then forced out a laugh and said he didn't know what I was talking about. I never saw him again. A week later, his apartment was empty, and a book-shaped package had been crammed through my letterbox.

I was cautious when I peeled it open, not wanting to rip the wrapping. I had never been given a present before. I hoped there'd be some kind of clue, or note, but there was nothing. The dictionary sat there, a glossy hardback threatening to burn a hole in my carpet. I cut a recess in my mattress for it and buried it there, convinced the army were going to come for me. In many ways, it really was just a normal book. It seemed ordinary, with its small print and flimsy white pages. Reading it was like slipping into the bath when it's cold and raining outside. It made me feel warm, and a little light-headed, and a little bit sick. I couldn't stop thinking about it. I checked on it endlessly, hoping to catch the changes in action, but I never saw a thing.

Strange, though, how I started to forget the old word meanings, and how quickly everything changed. I couldn't just stop going to work, but I found leaving the house much harder, because the world outside seemed so dull. The colour had leaked out of the sky, and everything felt grey and heavy. My work wasn't great but it wasn't bad either, hours and hours of fixing up army uniforms, washing the blood and other fluids out and folding them up into neat packages for the new recruits. I used to be okay with it because it was solid work, the kind that kept me out of trouble. But then I read the book and started hating the drudgery.

I have read the book so many times now, some of the definitions are seared into my brain. Take this word: *ease*. I say it like an exhale, gently pushing it through my teeth.

Ease
/iːz/

NOUN

A harmonious world free from the fear of punishment, oppression or prejudice. Not a utopia, which implies this world is imaginary and therefore unachievable, but a world that is being willed into arrival at this very moment.

1. The state of rising from your bed each morning knowing you will return to it unscathed by violence.
   'I went about my day with ease!'

2. The act of reassuring someone all will be well in this new world; and that none shall be left behind.
   'Friend, let me put your mind at ease.'

That last line – *friend, let me put your mind at ease* – brings tears to my eyes. I do not know this feeling, but I miss it desperately. I wonder if my parents, before they were disappeared, had ever known it.

Another word I think about often, when I'm at the factory and the bleach from the uniforms makes the skin on my hands crack, is *theft*.

Theft
/θɛft/

NOUN: theft; PLURAL NOUN: thefts
The action taken by governments, institutions, groups or individuals to exploit other human beings, other animals, or natural resources. The act of stealing autonomy and power from others to feed it back to the status quo, which a) perpetuates inequality, b) divides us and c) convinces us that we have no say in how the world functions.
'The government is committing theft when it refuses to ensure everyone has the basic requirements to live healthily and freely.'

It's been months now since Sid left, and the world is still changing. They stopped reading new words almost as soon as they started. Now they report unceasingly on the book burnings, and the people who get caught in possession of one. They are all forcibly conscripted, sent to the front lines in Europe. I can't seem to find much fear in me, though. I live alone; no one knows I have one too. I go to work every day and then I stay home. I stay home and I read, and everything changes.

The same day I re-learn *backlash*, some of the neighbours decide to break curfew again, gathering outside
our apartment block for a little party. I keep the blinds
drawn and do not go down there, even when I hear them
singing and smell the tantalising sweetness of freshly
baked cinnamon bread. They are quiet, and it's just a
handful of people, but somebody reports them anyway.
They have been out there for barely an hour when two
army trucks come barrelling down the narrow, pothole-
riddled road and men surround them like an oil spill.
I don't see it, no one sees it, because everyone stays
away from their windows when these things happen.
Looking out the window risks one of two disasters. The
first is that one of the officials glances up, sees your
face and throws you in with the rest. The second is that
everyone thinks you're the rat that got the neighbours
disappeared. In both cases, you're dead.

We all hear it happen, though. They are arrested and
removed so quickly and methodically, it's like they never
existed in the first place.

I don't see them again.

Backlash
/ˈbaklaʃ/
NOUN: backlash; PLURAL NOUN: backlashes
Waves of fury emanated by those fearful of the
rapid dismantling of power dynamics that requires
them to give up positions of status, wealth,
authority or influence, in order to ensure everyone
else has the right to access those things too.

Deployed at pivotal moments of change to trick you into thinking everything is getting worse. The truth is, everything is getting better.

'Throughout history, backlash has been a predictable response to radical progression, or to those demanding to be treated equally. Sometimes, equality means the simple right to joy.'

That night fractures everything beyond repair. I always thought my neighbours protected each other from the stink of the outside, however we could. That had been my block: poor, bitter, but never vindictive. But that had changed, too.

Within a few days of the disappearances, a body is dumped outside in the same spot where the party had taken place. It hits me by surprise when I step out in the morning to begin my long walk to work. The summer heat has made the body swell and the stench makes me gag so intensely my eyes water. I cross the street, and, just in case anyone is watching, I don't look closely enough to identify who could have possibly betrayed us. When I come back that evening, the body is gone and the sidewalk is clean, like it never happened in the first place.

Not long after this, they roll out the army to barricade us in. Armed men stand out in the streets and watch us like they're bored and need an excuse. No one can leave except to go to work. They shut down the supermarket and start to distribute food packages to each house, which contain vitamins instead of fruit and vegetables. Fresh apples were one of the few things we had left to enjoy; their absence makes me sad. At first, I think we're being punished for the murder, but then the news tells us it's because of the girls. The definition of 'girls' changed a few days ago, and some kind of seismic shift happened, when all of us here were distracted by shock and mourning.

The news tells me the girls are running wild. Packs of girls, some as young as five, are roaming the streets in the big cities, singing and dancing at three in the morning and fighting with the armed men. Quite a few of them are carrying weapons, weapons they know how to use. The thought of it stuns me so much that I do the only thing that makes sense; I reach for the dictionary.

When I read the new version of *girl*, I fall in love with it. I read it again before I go to sleep, and then one more time in the morning. I mutter it under my breath like a prayer, like a song.

Girl
/geːl/
NOUN: girl; PLURAL NOUN: girls

1. Eternal warriors of joy
   'Have you ever sat amongst young girls and listened to how funny and how brilliant they are?'

2. Harbingers of doom
   'I saw a group of girls outside, and they were armed and covered in blood.'

3. Undoers of the old world
*'The girls have declared that there is no room left for
power-hungry despots who rule by destruction.'*

I spend most of my Saturday lying on the floor with
my feet propped up against the wall, swallowing vitamin
tablets and rolling the words around in my mouth. I
desperately want to be the new, more exciting version of
girl. I worry that I am too old, too much of the before
times, too slow to change. I worry that being desperately
unhappy but too timid and lonely to go outside and join
them prohibits me from becoming *girl*.

I fall asleep and dream of a huge pack of girls, their
hair rippling and bouncing as they run together like a
river-flow. They come up, up through our apartment
block and start pounding on doors and sniffing us out.
They burst into my bedroom and many little hands
scrabble to pick my limbs up. I dream they are carrying
me out and the sky above is clear in the way it hasn't
been in my lifetime. I can see millions and millions of
stars. In the dream I'm not the only one being held up by
them. Others who want to be *girl* are also being carried
on this current of tangled hair, small feet and toothy
grins. In the dream, I cry with joy, for the first time ever.

And when I wake up, sweaty, with my pillow wet and
my mouth dry, I hear strange noises outside. Whoops
and cheers and high-pitched squeals that sound like
nothing I've really heard before. I am cautious at first,
peering through the blinds carefully, but then I get a
glimpse of the carnage below and I rush out to my tiny,

creaking balcony, to see it more clearly. I am not the only one; many familiar faces reflect my shock back at me.

All those grown men lie dead: their brains beaten in; or their limbs torn apart and neatly piled up next to their torso; or their hearts literally pulled from their chests, lying beside them in a mess of blood and gore. Their guns are gone, and around them, ten or so girls jump from tank to tank like kittens. Some of them are still wearing their pyjamas. They are armed and covered in blood. It is one of the best and worst things I have ever seen. I stare down at them and wonder how on earth they could have killed thirty men so quickly and efficiently. It feels like the whole building is holding its breath. I think about what their little limbs are capable of, and what Sid would make of all this. I think he'd be happy. I wonder what they will do with us. I look down and every time my eye settles on one, I think, *girl*, and then *girls, girls, girls, girls, girls, girls*, feeling like I've swallowed too much air and it's stuck in my ribs.

One of the girls looks up and spots me. Now I can smell the blood in the air. But we make eye contact and then she waves. She's wearing her pyjamas: a white cotton tank with little teddy bears embroidered on them, and matching shorts. I don't think she can be older than eight. I'm so nervous I'm shaking, but I wave back, and she gives me a sweet smile.

'WAIT THERE!' she shouts, and takes off running, dragging an AR-15 behind her. The gun's barrel scrapes the ground as she disappears around a corner. I squat down, grip the metal railings as if they will hide me and watch the girls as they play amongst the bodies. Some of them climb into the tanks and pretend to drive them, and others go through the pockets of the dead men, searching for supplies.

One of them is so young she shocks me. No older than five. I watch her crouch beside a body and examine it with the confident curiosity of a child, an unsteady finger reaching out to poke through the soldier's skull, which has burst open. Hunched up like that, she seems so uncoordinated and small, I can't imagine how she could have gripped a weapon, let alone used it. As I watch, she plunges her hand right into his head, behind his ear, and wriggles it around, screeching in delight. She loses interest quickly though. I watch her remove her hand and push a bloody, brain-covered thumb into her mouth. I watch her pat the man's sunken cheek with her free hand.

I am so entranced by her, I do not see the girl with the teddy bear pyjamas running back around the corner and darting into our block of flats. So when there's a pounding at my door, I jump so forcefully I slam my forehead painfully into the metal railings, scraping off some of the skin. When I take a scrambling look into the peephole, all I can see is the barrel of a rifle and the very top of a little brown head of hair.

When I open the door, she is panting, and so pleased with herself she starts talking before I've even realised what she's pushing into my arms.

'I've got you a whole crate,' she says. 'I can get more – for the whole building if you want!' Her arms are slippery with blood, and I see what I think might be brain matter smeared into her scalp. Her rifle is propped up against my doorframe.

I stare down at the box in awe, filled to the brim with red apples, and inhale their sweet, cidery scent. 'How did you—'

She bursts into giggles and hops from one foot to the other, scratching at her matted hair. 'I like apples! I hope you like apples too! But if you don't like apples, I can probably find you something else. Don't worry!'

Behind me I start to hear sirens, the drone of copters. Instinctively, I grip the apple-box tighter, wonder what is going to happen now. *Girl* just watches me and grins and grins and grins and grins.

Harmless, But Profoundly Irritating

Moira was busy tipping the salt into the sugar jar and the sugar into the salt jar when the doorbell rang.

'I'm not getting it!' she yelled as Alan shuffled to the door, a packet of frozen peas held up to his temple. She hadn't *meant* for the saucepan to hit him, per se, more to startle him with the noise it would've made when it clattered to the ground.

It hadn't been an easy feat, gluing the pan to the ceiling. She could still feel – still fall – despite what had happened to her. Moira had had to drag a ladder out from the shed and draw a wobbly circle in gorilla glue around the pot, holding it up there until her arms ached. A button on her favourite cardigan snagged on the ladder as she descended, and it had ripped clean off, so she was quite annoyed when the pot came unstuck almost immediately the next morning. It fell on her husband's head unexpectedly, clipping him around the head and making him yelp.

'God*dammit!*' he'd shouted, slamming his hand on to the counter and rubbing his temple as the pan rolled away. She'd briefly worried about him, but it was brilliant to see the confusion on his face as he stared at the kitchen ceiling. Even Alan couldn't do the mental gymnastics to work out this one. Quite uncharacteristically, he decided to call the doctor. As Moira listened to him, she tried her best to feel guilty.

'I looked up and – and a *pan* was stuck on the kitchen ceiling,' he said down the phone, 'and I was trying to get it down with a broomstick when it fell on me. The handle caught my temple.'

Silence on the other end of the line. 'You idiot,' Moira said loudly. 'You sound absolutely bonkers – the doctor's not going to see you *now*.'

'I might have a concussion,' her husband added. If he heard her – she knew he probably hadn't – he gave no sign.

The doctor told him he'd pay him a visit within the hour. And now here he bloody was, ringing their doorbell.

It had all started with a teapot falling off the counter. Well, not exactly falling. Moira had knocked it off deliberately when Alan had ignored her the fourth time she asked if he wanted a cuppa. He hadn't even turned around!

The teapot had shattered, naturally, when she'd pushed it, and her husband had started, spilling tea on to his thigh. Quite a satisfactory response, really. Moira had waited, with her hands on her hips, as she watched him pick up china fragments, staring from the door to the window in confusion. 'Must've been a draught,' he muttered, setting the teapot handle on to the counter. He'd left the rest on the floor, where it would remain for almost a week. The teapot had been a wedding gift, bright yellow with a huge daisy on the lid. She'd always thought the shade of yellow looked like vomit. But even all that mess and fuss hadn't been enough for him to acknowledge her presence.

'You're an absolute twerp, Alan,' Moira had said, as he settled back down on the sofa without so much as a glance her way.

This had been happening so often lately that Moira at first worried he was losing his hearing, or his memory. He was the sort of man who waved off these kinds of concerns, so he didn't bother following it up. And as it turned out, he didn't need to. It soon became apparent it was *only* Moira who he was ignoring. And it wasn't just him. The friendly pharmacist with beautiful, curly hair, who once slipped a packet of lemon lozenges into her paper bag with her blood pressure pills, barely looked at her now. Only the week before, the waitress in her favourite local hadn't taken her order for the best part of an hour. And strangers on the bus kept crashing into her; one man even tried to sit in her lap once before jumping up in alarm when she yelled at him. Moira was not a patient woman at the best of times. Once she figured it out, she went straight to her doctor – the same one now bothering them at home – to warn him that she was turning invisible.

Alan finally got the door open and ushered Dr What's-His-Face into the living room. She hovered behind them as they shook hands. The doctor was so focused on Alan he didn't notice when she stole the hat off his head and placed it on to her husband's. Unbelievable. At least Alan registered the switcheroo and quickly tossed the hat on to the table in the hallway.

As he boiled the kettle, fussed with the teabags and got the milk out, Moira watched the doctor observe him carefully, glancing around the house. In one hand he held a stupid little notebook. She hated it, and she hated that he was here, interrupting her plans.

She'd been extra careful when she'd gone to his office that day, wearing her pearls, her wool coat and a bright red scarf to look presentable, and not like an old, mad woman wasting the time of a doctor young enough to be her son. But it hadn't worked. Perhaps she'd have had a better chance if she'd got her kit off. He'd barely glanced at her in that nasty cotton-poly-blend shirt of his, and then turned to his computer screen. Moira followed his eye to the top left, where her date of birth was, with a sinking feeling. These days, everyone spoke to Moira like she was stupid or helpless; an escaped lamb that needed to be corralled back to the pen. She'd watched the doctor calculate her age and then gently take her hand with his limp, clammy one. The feeling had disgusted her, and she'd had to resist the urge to pull away. Pity has a grating edge to it, and she felt as if she was pressed right up against a razor blade, shaving little bits of her flesh off.

'How are things at home, Moira?' Dr What's-His-Face asked in the softest, most condescending manner. He was trying to look into her eyes but couldn't quite pin them down. The colour had been reduced to a watery nothingness.

'Alan can still get it up, if that's what you're asking.'

'Er . . . no, no, that's not what I was asking. I mean, how are things with *you*?'

Moira had stared disgustedly at the mustard stain on his tie, and decided there and then that she wasn't going to go quietly. 'D'you know what, Brian, or whatever your name was – things are fine with me. My back hurts, but it's been hurting since I was about forty. I'm the same as I've always been. It's everyone else that's decided I'm a problem.'

'It's Richard. And is that why you feel like you're, erm,' he glanced at his little notepad, 'turning invisible?'

The entire conversation was getting on her nerves. 'I don't *feel* like I'm turning invisible, I quite literally *am* turning invisible. It's happening right now – you can't even look at me properly.'

'And do you think this could be to do with what you mentioned earlier, about you and your husband's, um, bedroom time? Do you feel maybe that he's not giving you the attention that would meet your needs?'

Moira had really had to stop herself from telling her doctor to fuck off. 'You know something? People really shouldn't wear clothes with plastic in them, like polyester. It makes them stink.'

Now, seeing him sitting on her sofa, she snuck up behind him and quickly, confidently, grabbed a fistful of his hair. Tugged it hard. She chuckled as he yelped in surprise, dropped his pen and leapt up from his seat.

'What the hell was that?

'I'm so sorry – it must have been the cat. He's nervous around strangers. Are you all right?' her husband said hastily.

Moira was impressed – they didn't have a cat.

'I suppose . . . yes, I'm fine.' Frowning, the doctor rubbed the back of his head. He sighed. Old people were always the most complicated.

'I was just making myself a cup of tea. Can I get you one?'

'Thank you, Alan, that would be lovely. Two sugars, please.' Behind him, Moira twisted her hands together in excitement. The thrill of it all! The potential for mischief! For revenge!

At first, her transition to utter and complete invisibility was agonisingly slow. The opposite of fire, the antithesis of frenzy. But it was still rage. Sometimes, rage is quiet. The feeling of being transparent instilled such a fury in her that she stayed up most nights, pacing back and forth in front of the big mirror in the hallway, hoping to catch the moment where she'd finally disappear entirely. People spoke over her in the shops, edged around her impatiently in the streets, and laughed when she told them she felt opaque. And then, one day, she'd woken up with the sun on her face – no, *through* her face. Next to her, her husband of more than thirty years looked over and frowned, as if trying to remember who had once occupied that side of the bed. Moira had watched the memory of her drain out of his eyes and felt the weight of herself vanish, like a round, smooth pebble, sinking into darkness.

It had been strange at first, and quite upsetting. Moira was not a flappable woman by most people's standards, but this had really shaken her. She'd drifted around the house in a state of shock, too scared to go beyond the garden in case she disintegrated into nothing. For weeks she mourned, until that became boring, and Moira decided to have some fun with it all.

Only yesterday, she'd squeezed out all the toothpaste from the tube into a large pile in the sink, like a minty dog turd. Then she'd ripped little holes in the corner of every teabag in the cupboard too, laughing as Alan swore and dumped out one cup of tea after the other.

'Must have been a defective box,' he'd muttered, pulling on his coat. Poor Alan floated between denial and despair as his home slowly turned against him. Sometimes, out of the corner of his eye, he thought he caught movements: the wriggle of a toe or the bend of the knee. Once, when daydreaming, he thought he heard a laugh that belonged to someone he once knew. But it was like trying to follow the path of a fly zooming around the room; eventually, his eyes glazed over.

His wife watched him failing to see her and began stuffing all his left socks down the backs of the radiators.

Moira had so many ideas. They filled her with a giggly kind of glee. Encasing his slippers in ice! Poking holes in all the eggs and letting them seep down the fridge door! Once she'd properly got going, it became easier and easier to let go, until she felt like she'd jettisoned a lifetime's worth of emotional baggage. All that was left was a childlike delight. And that terrible anger, of course. That one seemed to be a permanent resident within her.

And now, as Dr What's-His-Face peered and prodded at her husband's forehead, Moira filled his coat with muddy stones she'd gathered from the garden. She took great care to smear dirt along the cuffs of his coat sleeves as the men discussed the ceiling pot incident. Despite his occasional buffoonery, Moira's husband was at least sharp enough to recognise what happened when people his age began to talk about things no one else understood. By the time the doctor was done, he'd thought of a suitable lie.

'I must've been shaken when we spoke earlier – I said something about it being on the ceiling, didn't I! It was just stuck on the top shelf, you see, and I couldn't quite reach it. I'll have to get one of those little stepladders.' He forced a laugh.

Nodding in approval, Moira popped a snail into the coat's breast pocket. And then one more, for good measure. She wondered if there was any fox poo left out on the lawn that she could add.

Brian had just taken a sip of tea. For a moment he held the liquid in his mouth as the saltiness hit, and wondered if he could get away with spitting it back into the cup. But Alan was watching him nervously, waiting to see if his story would hold up. Painfully, he swallowed, looking around the room to conceal his grimace.

'It's quite a place you've got here.' The doctor realised that all the pictures were hung upside down.

He noted the dust lining the shelves, the clock displaying the wrong time, and the fact that his patient's slippers were wedged high up in the curtain rail. Eventually he asked, in a special, gentle voice he reserved for the very young and the very old, 'How long have you been living alone, Alan?'

Her husband looked perplexed. 'Oh, not long. I was married to a perfectly fine woman, but she's . . . not been around for a few years.'

Moira snorted. 'I've been gone a few *months*, you idiot.'

'A couple of years is a long time to be living by yourself. There's no need to rush, but have you thought about an assisted living facility? There's usually a waiting list, so it might be something to consider sooner than you'd think.'

Moira blew into his ear. 'This is a VERY boring conversation. I think Alan's pretty content with how things are, don't you agree?'

Alan was shifting unhappily in his seat. 'Yes, I could have a think about it,' he said limply.

'I'll send a few brochures to you in the mail.' The doctor stood up and started to search for his coat. 'And in the meantime, take care of yourself, okay, Alan?'

As soon as Brian left, bemused by how dirty his coat was, she went right back to it. There were all sorts of things she hadn't crossed off her list yet – today, she planned to crumble a packet of spaghetti into ever-smaller bits. After the soaps, of course. Tomorrow, she would tear up the roots of the flowers she had once watered so fastidiously. Maybe she'd throw the soil around and smear it into the ground to spell out something obscene on the pavement. Debbie from next door would really hate that – she always got prissy and squeaky whenever Moira swore in front of her. Then there was the prized bottle of sherry which she could replace with balsamic vinegar, and on Wednesday she had pencilled in ripping every fifth page out of all the books – except her favourites, of course.

Alan had taken to swearing at the empty rooms and, eventually, talking loudly to the air as if he sensed his wife was behind the chaos in the house. Once, he shouted, 'Stupid woman!' in the living room when he couldn't find the remote. In response, Moira pulled all the buttons off his shirts and hid them in the oven.

It probably could have continued forever. But a few weeks in, she started to grow a little bored. There is a limit, after all, to the chaos you can cause if no one else is there to appreciate it.

And then Wednesday evening rolled around.

The TV was showing the eight o'clock special, when Moira heard the news reporter say something about 'poltergeists and supernatural occurrences happening across the country'. She ran over to the settee where Alan was perched with his newspaper, and sat down heavily next to him. He muttered something about needing more room; she ignored him and turned up the volume.

The reporter was chic in her navy dress, young and glowing with life. Moira instantly liked her. She adjusted her black-frame glasses and continued, 'An unusual interest in the ghostly and the occult has gripped the nation in recent days, as reports flood in about strange things happening in homes and care facilities, parks and hospitals.' She cleared her throat. 'The most common of these . . . incidents involve things falling off shelves and slamming doors . . . harmless pranks, really. Although some people have reported minor injuries – including two men that required hospital visits.'

Moira's hands were pressed to her mouth, a tremor of excitement running through her, but at that she let out a guffaw. 'See that, Alan? I could have landed you in the hospital, but I didn't! Count yourself lucky!'

The scepticism was rolling off the reporter like sweat, but she tried her best to sound professional. 'We've received video footage capturing what people are calling "poltergeists" on camera, but I'll let you be the judge of that.' The screen cut to a series of clips from shaky home videos.

And there they were! Flowers being ripped from the ground, bags of flour suddenly flung to the floor, toilet paper unravelling, or even entire tables flipped over – and in the background, there were the older women laughing, scowling, shouting and crying, their limbs like cellophane, unable to catch the light. The other people in the clips were yelling in confusion and alarm, searching for answers – some of them even ran right through the women in their panic. The phones shook, the women seemed to blur with the air – but Moira could see them all. She felt their heat surging through the screen. Others! Having fun! Angry! Just like her! Her chest thumping, she watched each clip and tried to commit each woman to memory. 'This whole time, I thought I was alone,' she said out loud. She was surprised at the weight of her voice and how solid it felt.

Her husband, meanwhile, glanced around the room nervously. 'Jesus Christ,' he mumbled, shrinking a little into the sofa cushions. Ordinarily, she would have responded to this feeble acknowledgement with a playful ruffle of the hair, or blown cold air down his neck, but she couldn't tear her gaze from the TV, where the reporter was now back on-screen, leaning forward on her elbows.

'Of course, we should take this all with a healthy pinch of— OW!' The young woman suddenly leapt up from her seat in shock, rubbing the back of her neck. She focused on someone off-camera and mouthed, 'Something just pinched me!'

Moira was howling with laughter – because she'd seen her coming! Clear as day! The woman, at least ninety, stood behind the reporter with a look of pure glee on her face.

'There's your salt!' she yelled triumphantly into the reporter's lapel mic. With a wave, the old woman walked out of the camera's view, laughter still lingering behind her.

Council of Dead Women

A lot of our newest members think we're witches, but we're not, and sometimes this disappoints them. I get it. I first thought that too, when I pushed open the ancient wooden doors – light as a slap – to see fourteen strange-looking women with their green skin, welcoming me to the fold. I wouldn't have minded being a witch, after all that I'd been through. But I've heard the Council's spiel so many times now, I've kind of bought into it myself: witches are made *by* the earth as weapons, and we're born *from* it as guardians, which isn't quite the same thing.

These days, women pour into our halls as if a dam has burst. Many of them don't know they're dead yet. We have to break it to them. Those moments are the hardest, because when they understand they almost always know who killed them and why, and they seem to lose all shape, spilling on to the floor like a burst blood vessel. When it happens, there's rarely a dry eye in the chamber. When it happens, we gather around with quiet love and gently help the woman to her feet again.

The Council came into being at the very birth of humanity, when the first men killed the first women and let their bones sink into the earth to be chewed up and swallowed. The earth, being less than neutral in this situation, did not comply. The bones were gathered up instead and re-spun into the First Fourteen. Mud and moss replaced their flesh and banana leaves bound their limbs together. Whenever I tell the arrivals this story, I wait for one of them to ask about the smell. Because that's what I can't stop thinking about – how pungent things must have been when they all got together. Mud *stinks*. But so far, no one's asked, and now I've been here for too long to do it myself.

Since the birth of the Council, there have been seven core members and seven revolving ones, to ensure experience was delicately balanced with new rage. We put hours and hours into planning and arranging and checking in with each other to make sure no one works too hard for too long. You can imagine the paperwork! Dealing with mortality is a difficult enough job for the living, let alone the dead – but now it's my turn, I'm excited to try. This decade I've been assigned to minuting the meetings. I'm pretty pleased – it's not often that a newbie like me gets chosen for such an important role. In fact, I thought I wouldn't get the chance, because ever since I died my memory and focus haven't been very good – it's the brain damage, you see. But I told the Department for Occupations Beyond the Grave that I'd be up to it, and they respected me enough to listen. Plus, it means I'll be one of the few in the room where the magic happens, and won't it make me popular at the dinner table! I'll be damned (ha!) if I don't have my turn to greet the new members and help them process their new reality.

It's a terribly disorienting thing, actually, because you don't always remember what happened to you. The body is also vastly transformed. I mean, for one thing, we're all tinged with green, which a lot of new members find troubling. For some of them it's the most shocking part – they assume they've been drugged and have woken up in a cult. Or that they're just in a very long, very boring nightmare which essentially consists of lots of oddly dressed women wandering around, asking them how they're feeling. I get it, though. I've only been here a decade or two and still have trouble adjusting. Not from the killing – from the living.

Eli was both a stunning artist and a horrifically violent man and I was his favourite canvas. We met in the stupidest way possible – I was twenty-two and working as one of those princesses for hire, and he had just started a job as a live portrait artist. You know, the kind that paints a wedding scene as it takes place? We met at this obscenely rich kid's thirteenth birthday party, and I was Princess Esmeralda, with the green dress and little tiara. I had sweat pouring down my face from my cheap wig, and he looked like he wanted to shoot himself. He painted me into the picture, and we left together and I never looked back. I still have the dents from where he smashed my skull in, but they're fading. I could, if I wanted to, choose to forget it altogether – but very few of us do. We need the memories to help the new ones, you see.

Like the woman we are welcoming in now. Or should I say, girl. The bell out in the hall is ringing to let us know she's ready to come in, and someone from the Department of Process and Procedure has already entered the adjudication room to hand out her file. Running the Council is a huge logistical tangle, I tell you. We've got over sixty different departments – including the Department of Departments, which makes sure all the others are doing all right – covering every aspect of the afterlife for women like us.

I can almost smell the distress coming off her when she walks into our spacious, softly lit room. She's only fifteen. They've explained this whole Council business to her already; we've got specially trained members who give them all the time and space they need to process. Sometimes it's hours, even days. Other times, like today, they only need a few minutes. This girl, in her faded pink jumper and thin leggings, seemed to be expecting her death, which saddens me greatly.

Maia, today's co-chair, speaks first. 'Welcome, Beatriz,' she says gently, drawing her name out, like *Be-at-riz*, as if we are all there to sing this girl to full strength again.

'How are you feeling today?'

'I . . . um. I'm sorry if I'm being rude, but what the fuck is going on?'

Beatriz reminds me of a baby bird, with her wide eyes and hands clasped to her chest. She's busy examining each of the fourteen Councilwomen with a slightly dazed look on her face. This is normal. We have seen every possible reaction over the years, but confusion is the default. I remember standing where she stood, shivering and convinced it was all a dream as the Council explained things to me. I'd always had an impressive imagination – it was why I wanted to be a writer, before.

Maia smoothly moves on to the welcome speech that I've now heard hundreds of times. I watch her silver and turquoise earrings swing back and forth with the movement of her head. She's kind, and always patient, one of the permanent women who co-chairs the Council. She'll do a maximum of fifty years (union mandate) and then someone else – maybe someone like me – will replace her. The only rule of this place that we can't change is that once you're here, you don't leave. There is nowhere else to go.

'I understand this may be a lot to process right now,' Maia is saying softly, 'so if you need some time, that's all right with us.' She pushes her hair out of her face, a green so dark it's like the sea is hugging her shoulders. 'We are known as the Council of Dead Women. We've been here since the start, since the first man killed the first woman and the earth took note. We are here to welcome you to the afterlife and ease your journey into it. There are many things we can offer you, but the most important thing for you to know is that here you are both free and safe. This world is not against you.' She pauses and turns to her co-chair, Akinyi, who is seated next to her.

The rumour is that Akinyi is the eldest – older than all of us in this room combined, maybe. I've always wanted to ask her age, but it would be considered impolite. Her hair, piled in an elegant twist on the crown of her head, is dark enough to resist the green tinge that creeps up on all of us. She's on her forty-ninth year on the Council and has eyes so deep with compassion it's almost painful to look into them. It's like she draws out every moment you ever felt your heart break and siphons it away, until you feel fresh and hollowed out. Not everyone likes it, because many women still need to carry the hurt with them to grieve. Some grieve forever.

'Welcome, child. This is where you can talk through what it is you might need,' Akinyi explains in her slow, soporific voice. 'And what it is we can help you with.'

'What if you can't help me?' Beatriz whispers, her gaze firmly on her hands. Her nails are long and painted a sparkling purple, with tiny silver stars. I can see pink hearts glued to each of her thumbs. She must have sat in the salon for hours to get these done. On the bright side, though, she'll have them forever now, if she likes. That seems like the kind of thing a fifteen-year-old would be pleased about. I scribble *nails!* on the side of my notepad so I'll remember to pass that on later.

'Trust me. We can always help.' Akinyi turns to me and smiles. We try not to do hierarchy in the Council, so all fourteen of us are seated on one side of a long table, like the world's strangest job interview. Sometimes – although I wouldn't say this out loud – it gets a bit silly. For example, every time one of us needs to look at someone else, we have to crane our heads forward to try and catch her eye. Personally, I think it would be easier if we all sat in a circle on the floor or something. Maybe on some giant cushions, with some candles and— 'Gloria, would you mind running through the services we offer?'

I take a deep breath. 'Oh, well, there are so many I'm not even sure where to begin. We've got a department for everything – it's great! There's Counselling, of course, and then there's Spirit Recovery, Haunting for Hire, Telling, Adjustment, Funeral Dispatch, Human Liaison Services . . .'

Beatriz immediately looks overwhelmed. She's so young, so small in the centre of the room, her death still wringing its hands around her neck. I have to catch myself and slow down a little bit.

'Sorry, Beatriz – let me start over. We are here today to help you make some decisions. Or, if you're not ready to make any decisions, to present you with the full list of the options we have, so that when you are ready, you have all the information you need.'

'But what if I don't want to make a decision?'

'You don't need to do anything you don't want to,' Akinyi tells her. 'You can, if you prefer, remain in this stage you are in now. We do have women who make this choice, but if they stay stuck in this hallway, between death and afterlife, I'm afraid there are consequences beyond our control. If you stay here for too long, you will end up forgetting everything. Not just what happened to you, but who you are, your loved ones – everything. And once that happens, you will be unable to pass through those doors over there.' Here, Akinyi points to the set of doors behind her that are, unhelpfully, identical to the doors Beatriz came through. I've always thought we should paint them white or something, just to differentiate them a little. We all know what's on the other side, but to the new arrivals it probably looks very underwhelming.

What Akinyi doesn't add is that the lost souls wandering the hallways out there also disintegrate physically. Their bodies break down until all you can see are their souls, catching the light like shimmery veils wafting in the breeze. When you walk past them, you can sometimes hear them trying to speak. It's like putting your ear to a conch shell and trying to decipher the sound. Most women make a decision, once we explain this to them. I think it would be terribly lonely to be one of those souls, watching us all pass through, unable to follow. The best thing about this place is the community we have created to make the horror of what killed us a bit easier to bear. I can't imagine not being a part of it now.

'But many of us need a transition period before we can truly let go of the lives that were taken from us,' Maia is saying. She again turns to Akinyi and waits for her to pick up where she left off – that's another thing about the Council. We try not to monopolise the conversation and let others who wish to speak have their chance too.

'Gloria will run through the services she just mentioned again, and you can come back at any time if you want to know more, or even if you just need to talk.'

At that point, Beatriz looks up right into Akinyi's eyes. Her small hands, still twisted around the centre of her chest, loosen a little. I think that is where he stabbed her, before he crushed her neck. She nods and whispers something that might have been thanks. I'm not sure. One of the most important things in the chamber is learning how to read the women we serve. Too much information can overwhelm, too little can arouse suspicion. Trauma is sticky, like molasses, and has a tendency to get into every crevice and crack of the soul. Not everyone that comes our way is welded to it, of course, and for many of us it's a process of shrugging the past off like shedding skin, moving on to a different kind of existence. A lighter one. Not that it's easy, I tell you. But the point is, trauma is a tricky thing to manage, and it takes many years of practice to learn how to read terror. And I'm *great* at it.

Now is my time to shine.

'All right, Beatriz, I'm sorry if I spoke too fast earlier. Do you know what counselling is?'

She nods, so I keep going.

'Well, our Department of Counselling has many different types on offer. They're all designed with our experiences in mind, and they can help with the journey you're on right now. But on that journey, parts of us can get stuck in the in-between, usually because of something unresolved we've left back *there* in the other world. Which is why some people try the Department of Adjustment, and the Department of Human Liaison Services. See, with Adjustment, it's almost like going back to school, but there's no exams or anything like that. It's a chance to re-learn your history, your family's history, to dwell upon what led you to here. Not in a judgemental way – it's to help you accept that there's nothing you could have done to change the outcome of your life. None of this is your fault.'

I stop myself from telling her that although I chose acceptance, shortly after I arrived here, there is a whole department – the Department of Haunting for Hire – filled with women who decide never to let go. Instead, they choose to haunt the ones who brought them here. I'm tempted by that department from time to time, even though I've heard it's vaguely demonic. All the women who work there keep very tight-lipped about it, though.

'I like the sound of that,' Beatriz says, her eyes fixed on me. I can't help but notice her arms have lowered, and feel pride bloom in my chest. This is all I want, for her to feel like she can trust us.

'And we have the Department of Telling. That's a lovely one, it's all about learning the old stories women have held in their mouths for years and years. You can learn about the earth and what she did for us – some of the stories call her Gaia, others call her God or Goddess, or Lilith, or That Bloody Woman, or The Great Creator. Personally, I call her Terra.'

At this Beatriz lets out a sharp, nervous laugh, glancing around the room as if she thinks I'm making a joke. No one laughs, but Maia offers her a kind smile.

'There's also the Department of Mourning, which has an excellent service called Funeral Dispatch. That's when we send several former Council Members to attend your death rituals and preside over your body.

Some of us don't want anything to do with it, but others have deep religious or cultural ties to the corporeal of course, so our Councilwomen will record it all and step in if they need to. They also make sure Terra is able to take your body back and keep it safe, which is especially important if your body is in a place where it might not be found.'

I can sense a few of us watching Beatriz closely to see her reaction. The truth is that her body probably won't be found in time, judging by the way he disposed of it. Eli didn't even bother to hide mine. They found me the next morning at the bottom of the basement stairs, the blood a dried, dark brown. But Beatriz either hasn't realised it yet or is unfazed by the knowledge of where her body has been hidden. She looks exhausted, but calmer.

And so I plough on.

'And we also offer . . . we can help with . . .' But I'm tiring, scanning my notes to try and remember the rest of the services. Ever since I died, my memory and focus haven't been very good – it's the brain damage, you see. A warm hand squeezes my shoulder. Chiyoko has reached over and is gently rubbing my back. We've been close for years – I was thrilled when I found out we'd be on the Council duty together. She found me about six months into my journey here and came knocking on my bedroom door when she'd heard how I'd arrived. This happens often – we gravitate towards women who died in similar ways to us so we can be a little gruesome together, and compare battle scars.

'Do you want me to take over, Gloria?'

'Actually, that would be great.'

'Only if you don't mind?'

'No, no, really—'

'If you're sure?'

'I'm sure!'

'Gloria, do you need to take a minute?' Maia leans around Chiyoko, concerned. 'We can pause.'

But I wave them on. The last thing I want is to keep Beatriz waiting. So Chiyoko continues, 'You can of course learn about these in your own time. But I think you might be interested in our Human Liaison Services, hmm? You have a mother you're worried for, if I am correct.'

Beatriz is nodding furiously, more animated now. 'Yes, yes, my mom, she still lives with the man who killed me. She's going to be next. You have to help her. You can do that, right?'

'Well . . . we can, and we also can't,' Chiyoko says. She ties her long, juniper-tinged hair in a quick bun and pulls a red form out from her stack of papers. Red is for the HLS department, where it seems like Beatriz will need to go next. 'We have women on the ground who we communicate with, who can pay your mother a visit and offer her help.' She sees the look of horror on Beatriz's face and adds quickly, '*Without* him knowing. Our operatives are incredibly skilled. Their only goal is freedom and security for the women they work with. They have helped hundreds of thousands of us escape from violent situations, no matter how long it takes.'

Chiyoko holds up the form, which has the words *Human Liaison Application* stamped on the front.

'But what we can't do,' Akinyi interjects gently, 'is forcibly take Mom away, or hurt him in any way. At the end of the day, she makes that decision alone.' As she speaks, she slowly brushes her fingertips over the table like she's enjoying the smoothness of the wood. It's a gesture I've seen many times, when she's trying to soothe the women standing in front of her.

'But she needs help *now*. I've been here for hours, she could be dead already—' Beatriz is half-turning to the doors, her face in an awful twist of hope and fear, as if expecting – fearing – her mother will walk in and embrace her. 'Please,' she begs. 'This whole Council with your endless departments and weird rules, why can't you just stop him, instead of wasting time on me?'

The anguish emanating from her is potent enough to bring tears to my eyes, and I'm sure I'm not the only one. Inevitably, I think of my daughter. My baby. How could I ever be ready to leave her behind, stuck in a world that kills women with such stunning ease? I know Beatriz's pain. It's hard sometimes, to walk into a room designed to meet every need and soothe every bruise, every deep cut, but also confront the truth that for all our power, we are still not much help in the world of the living. Despite my years here, I still can't quite believe this place, and what it does for us. Even this young, glowing girl whose father stabbed her and then strangled her to death, put her body in a plastic bag and threw her into the river. We will give her the tools and she will decide what path she will take with them. Rage, despair, oblivion, acceptance, healing, helping, haunting, or nothing at all . . . She is entirely in control, maybe for the first time ever. Terra may have plucked the first of us from death undeserved and far too soon, and cradled us in her arms, but at least the Council have crafted something unbelievable from the loss.

'Time here doesn't correlate to the time of the living, Beatriz. It may have felt like hours to you, but things are moving much, much slower for her. Your mother is alive,' I say, and I hope it helps a little.

She remains unmoving, her back still to us. She stays like this for some time, and we watch over her grief and try our best to hold some of it for her. Many of the others are struggling to smother their anger at what this poor girl has endured, but I can smell the kindness radiating from Akinyi like sweet, soft bread, fresh out of the oven. And the delicious smell of the ground after the rainy season. She catches my eye, gives me a jerky nod of approval, and I find a small fire blazing in the rich, mossy green of my chest. There's no satisfying end here, I'm afraid.

Finally, Beatriz turns back to us, wiping the tears that have slipped, like beautiful little pearls, down her face. Hand outstretched, she approaches the table and takes the form from Chiyoko. She looks at each of the women as though she can see the stories they bring to the table and all of the waters they carry. Both Maia and Akinyi died young, after living with violent, abusive fathers. It is why they co-chaired today, and why, when the Council

273

adjourns for the day, they will find Beatriz and embrace her, and listen to her as she spills out her sorrow, her rage, and everything else in between. And Maia will cry with her, as Akinyi stands guard over them both, preserving that moment forever. But Beatriz has yet to discover this. So, she takes her time, examining each of the faces above her once again, the form held delicately between those sparkling nails. She looks less like a bird now, and more like a mouse, with the paper clenched in her hands that way and her eyes darting around. Finally, she comes to me. Our eyes meet and she gives me a very small smile. As if *she* is trying to comfort *me*.

'The green hair is pretty cool, you know,' Beatriz mumbles in Spanish. Our mother tongue. I smile and her eyes flicker to the door behind us. We watch her approach it. Just before her outstretched hand is about to touch the wood, she turns once again. We know this moment well. It usually happens at the end of a session – the women give us their heartfelt thanks for the support and the love.

Beatriz seems like she has more to get off her chest and so, we wait, we hold the space for her, as long as she needs us to.

'You know,' she says, 'I still don't understand what the *fuck* is going on.'

And with that, she is gone. No one says anything, but I think I see Indira's shoulders shaking with laughter, and I know I'm in trouble. I clamp a hand over my mouth, but a small snort escapes me, and suddenly the whole room is cackling and shrieking. I see Sheila with her head thrown back, Nayao wiping a tear from her face, her mouth open and delighted, and Maia slumped over the table, holding her ribs.

I don't know about you, but to me, a symphony of women in full-throated, belly-aching laughter is the most defiant, beautiful sound there is. It's because the sound of our joy is also the sound of hope, and if we needed to, I think we could do it forever.

Here's the thing with death; you have to laugh about it sometimes, otherwise all that is left are tears. Everything from the old life takes on a cloudy haze, like you're on a train looking out of a fogged-up window, barely able to see what lies beyond. And then our real selves, the ones beneath the masks we construct in order to survive, start to shine through like tiny rays of sunshine. Eventually, we will fill up the room with light.

Acknowledgements

This book has been the most fun to write. I'm grateful to you, the reader, for lending it your time. Thank you.

It takes a village to write a book, and I'm lucky enough to be a part of an excellent one. To my family, who champion me even when I'm at my most dull (complaining about writing instead of writing), thank you, I love you.

To Luka: I write every book hoping you'll read it. I love you.

To my witch-auntie, for the reiki and the laughter and the madness. I love you.

To my writer and poetry friends, thank you for the support, the guidance and the enthusiasm. I'm lucky to know you, and to read your work.

To the women in my life: Becca, for reading the early drafts; Helena, for teaching me to trust my sense of humour; Simi, for holding all the worries I spill. To Ruby, Lauren, Ray, Bea, Malin, Aimee and Kylie for keeping me sane and making me laugh. Thank you, I love you.

To Jamie, for being Jamie. Thank you, I love you.

To my agent, Abi, for supporting and reassuring me every step of the way, thank you.

To the greats: Carmen Maria Machado, Rachel Yoder, Angela Carter, Chimamanda Ngozi Adichie, Kamila

Shamsie, Leslie Jamison, Deborah Levy, Guadalupe Nettel, Saba Sams, Sheena Patel and more and more and more. Thank you for your impeccable writing, and the influence it has on mine.

To Penguin and the #Merky Books team, I am so, so thankful for your efforts and expertise. In particular, thank you to my editors, Ansa, Charlotte and Amy, for your patience and insight. Thank you to Laurie, the copy-editor Sarah-Jane, and to the wider #Merky team: Helen, Cameron, Lemara, Alice, Lydia and Linda.

And thank you to the unnamed, but no less valued, people who made this book happen. The cover artists, designers, editors, assistants, publicists, marketing co-ordinators, typesetters – and any other role that I don't necessarily see but deeply appreciate. I'm grateful for your part in this work, you have no doubt made it better.

Finally, thank you to Gwyneth Paltrow, for the clitoral inspiration.

PS – if you spotted a typo in this book, no you didn't.